PLAYING WITH THE DEAD

A Jo Wolfe Psychic Detective crime thriller

Book 5

© Wendy Cartmell 2020

Wendy Cartmell has asserted her rights under the Copyright, Design and Patents Act, 1988, to be identified as the author of this work.

This is a work of fiction. References to real places, real people, events, establishments, organisations, or locations, are intended only to provide a sense of authentication, and are used fictitiously. All other characters, incidents and dialogue are drawn from the author's imagination and are not to be construed as real.

ISBN 9798592150371

This edition published 2021.

For Nebula 697
Thank you for introducing me
to the world of gaming.
You gave me invaluable help. All and
any mistakes are my own, not yours.
Love you, son.

By Wendy Cartmell

Sgt Major Crane crime thrillers:
kindleunlimited

Crane and Anderson crime thrillers:
kindleunlimited

Emma Harrison mysteries
kindleunlimited

Supernatural suspense
kindleunlimited

All my books are in KINDLE UNLIMITED and available to purchase or borrow from Amazon.

Chapter 1

Are you an experienced gamer?
Why not turn your love of gaming
into a revenue stream?
How?
By being a gaming beta-tester.
You will need persistence and perseverance.
It's not for everyone - only the bravest
and the best need apply.
Can you beat Penumbra?

Callum rocked back in his gaming chair and re-read the post. Beta-testing of computer games was a gig he'd been trying to get into for the past year, without much success.

He had all the equipment he'd ever need. Gaming laptop that he'd paid for with a part-time job, Xbox, and PlayStation that he'd got as presents on past Christmases, both hooked up to a large tv at the end of his bed.

The trouble was that applying to be a beta tester took almost as much effort as playing the bloody games, he'd decided. He'd dabbled with producing his own video reviews of computer games on YouTube and people said he had a strategic mind and gave balanced assessments, cutting through the gaming hype. Maybe this time he'd be lucky. Not everyone would have found the post, as it was in a gaming forum on the deep web, which in itself wasn't for the faint hearted. So maybe the odds wouldn't be so stacked against him this time.

Penumbra. He contemplated the name and quickly checked the thesaurus on his phone. Shadow, half-shadow. Something to do with an eclipse. He guessed that was a fair enough name for a horror type game. What he liked was that Penumbra was a hybrid game, not just a horror and not just a fighting game. The best of both worlds.

For a moment he experienced a chill, the hairs on his arms stood and goosebumps appeared. A warning? A portent of disaster? Was there something with him in his bedroom? Callum looked around. Dark shadows were collecting in the corners of his room, which was only lit with a spotlight-type lamp on his desk. He shivered, convinced the air was getting colder.

Then the bedroom door swung open as if on its own.

Callum held his breath.

And there stood his dad, tapping his watch.

Blowing away his stupid anxiety, Callum glanced down at his laptop screen and saw it was nearly Midnight. Tomorrow was to be his last day in school. 'A' level exams were finished, coursework had been submitted and it was time to say goodbye to everyone and get his tee-shirt signed. Before long he'd be off to University to do a degree in computer studies.

'Sorry, Dad,' Callum said. 'I just got…'

'Carried away. Yes, I know.' His father smiled. 'The heating's gone off so it'll get cold pretty quickly.'

'No worries, I'll get off to bed now. Night,' Callum called.

'Night, son,' and the door closed behind his dad.

Callum pushed away the lock of hair that was hanging down and resting on his forehead and had the annoying habit of getting in his eyes. He guessed he'd have to have a haircut soon. Well, maybe before he went off to Uni. Tearing his thoughts away from university and the freedoms it would bring with it, he pressed 'send' on his application.

He wasn't really expecting it would come to anything, as this sort of thing was normally oversubscribed, but hey it would be pretty amazing if it did. All he could do was to keep his fingers crossed and wish.

As Callum climbed into bed, an old adage floated into his mind: *Be careful what you wish for* and he experienced a frisson of fear. After convincing himself, almost, that he was just being silly, he dropped off into an uneasy sleep.

Chapter 2

DI Jo Wolfe sat alone in her office, in Chichester police station, dressed in her usual dark trouser suit and white shirt. On her feet were a pair of white trainers, her normal footwear, unless attending something formal, such as meetings with her bosses, or press conferences. She was reliving the moment when she'd really thought her career in the police force was over. Not only had her and her team had to battle a malignant Kelpie, but also DCI Sykes, an insidious boss who had been out for Jo's blood, because of a slight he'd received from her father many years previously.

She relived the agonising meeting they'd had with the Chief Superintendent in the conference room. The four of them; Jo, DS Eddie Byrd, DC Jill Sandy, and Father Osian Price from Chichester Cathedral, were holding their collective breaths, awaiting their fate.

'I've decided...' the Chief had paused dramatically, 'to do nothing.'

The four had looked at each other in surprise. 'Nothing, sir?' Jo had managed to ask.

'That's right, nothing. You are all to carry on as normal, but I don't want the details of your escapades being talked about in the police station. Jo's gift and your battles with the supernatural will be our secret. When you take another case, you will work directly under my supervision. Got it?'

They had all nodded enthusiastically.

'I'm sure we can find lots of strange, weird and wonderful cases for you all to get to the bottom of. I'll assign them, but in the meantime carry on with closing down the missing men case.'

So, it was now up to Jo to talk to the remaining two members of her team, Sasha, and Ken. Sasha being Jo's computer whizz and Ken being a dogged investigator nearing retirement, solid and reliable. They'd had no new cases as yet, but there was still lots of work to do to wrap up the previous case, when Jo, Eddie, Jill and Osian had found the missing young men on Pagham Beach.

None of those rescued had regained their memories of their time spent goodness knows where, under the spell of the Kelpie. Each one had still to be interviewed again, their families talked to and the press dissuaded from making a mountain out of a molehill and printing reams of words that were nothing but speculation and supposition. But that was nothing new when it came to dealing with journalists. There was money to be made in the investigation of police cases. Pages of detailed exposure sold newspapers in the ever more cutthroat world that was print journalism. Digital media made life very hard for the newspapers and they fought back with everything they had. Investigative journalism was on the rise and the last thing Jo wanted was for a reporter to decide to get his or her teeth into one of their cases.

Jo needed to speak to Sasha and Ken to find out

if they were happy to continue to work under her. Sasha was a little different to the normal police officer, as she was happier in front of a computer and with as little interaction with humans as possible.

Jo called her into her office and Sasha huffed her irritation at the interruption, but left her desk and went to speak to Jo.

'Sasha, I need to speak to you about the future of this team.'

Jo paused as Sasha had gone pale. 'Have you decided to get rid of me?' she asked in a small voice, but then raised her head in defiance, that seemed to say, come on, give me your worst.

'What? No, of course not. Why would you think that?'

But, of course, Jo knew why Sasha would think that, after being pushed from pillar to post when she'd worked in other departments. She was literal, prickly, some would say self-absorbed and dismissive of those she felt were beneath her intelligence. On the other hand, she was meticulous, cared a great deal about her work, was autonomous and worked harder and faster than anyone Jo knew.

'It's just that we're leaving the mainstream Major Crimes and working directly for the Chief Superintendent from now on. After we've wrapped up the lost men case, of course.'

'Is that all?'

'What? Well, yes. I wanted to check that you

were happy with that.'

'Do I still get to work with you, Eddie and Jill?'

Jo nodded.

'That's fine then,' said Sasha and returned to her desk leaving Jo gaping in her wake.

Next was Ken. Older, wiser, yet still a DC. Jo wasn't sure what decision he'd make. She wasn't sure that Jo's unit was an exact match for Ken. But it was his decision not hers.

What he did say, surprised her.

'Thanks for the offer, but I've decided to retire.'

'Really? Why?'

'Because I'm over 60 and starting to get creaky. The wife has just taken early retirement and is pushing for me to join her. I could have gone 5 years ago but kept going. The early mornings, late nights and hours and hours spent out in the cold are taking their toll on me, and the wife and I want to buy a motorhome and tour around the UK in the summer and maybe even Europe in the winter.'

'Oh, Ken, that's marvellous!'

He looked at her. 'For who?'

Jo grinned. 'For you, you fool,' she said, and he smiled in reply.

'I've already filled out the paperwork,' he said. 'All I've to do now is to sign on the dotted line and after what you've just said, this is as good a time as any. I've enjoyed working with you and the rest of your team, boss, and wish you all the best.'

'And the same to you,' Jo said. 'We'll miss you

mind, especially Jill I expect. She's learned a lot from you.'

'She's shaping up to be a good detective and I hope she stays the course, what with getting married and such.'

Jo nodded. 'I hope so too, Ken. Let me know when you've a date sorted with Human Resources.'

'Of course, boss,' and Jo watched Ken walk away. She was sad to see him go, but his decision wasn't unexpected. And Marjory, his wife, would be delighted.

So, going forward it was to be Jo and Eddie as one pairing and Sasha and Jill the other. Whatever the next case brought, she hoped they could cope with it. Something told her that working on the fringes of Major Crimes might not be the most comfortable of places, but surely the most exciting.

Chapter 3

Callum peeled off his tee-shirt and looked at the scrawled autographs. They'd had a great last day and had run around the school and the grounds ferreting out friends and collecting signatures. He wondered how many names he'd remember in the years to come. Probably not that many, for university called and with it a new chapter in his life. He looked around his room that would be stripped bare in September and all his worldly goods exported to Cambridge. He'd had his offer letter that very morning, based on his projected grades, and it was pinned up in pride of place on his cork board. He touched it in disbelief. Getting into Oxbridge. How amazing was that? He idly wondered about joining the rugby team, or even the rowing club. Who knew, perhaps one day he could row in the Boat Race, that annual event where Oxford University were pitted against Cambridge University in the famous competition held on the River Thames in London.

But he was getting ahead of himself, he grinned. He still had to get the required grades in his exams. Still, idle speculation cost nothing. For now, he needed a shower and then food.

He'd just emerged from his bedroom, showered and changed into clean clothes, when his mother called, 'Oh there you are, Callum, there's a courier here for you.'

'A courier? For me? Are you sure?'

'Yes, come on, hurry up.'

Callum ran down the short flight of stairs, his bare feet making no sound on the thick carpet. It couldn't be. Surely not? Callum dismissed the thought of having been chosen as a beta player as nonsense. He'd only sent in his application late last night. It must be something else. One of his mates playing a prank on him maybe?

Waiting at the door was a figure dressed in dark motorcycle leathers and a full-face crash helmet with a blacked out visor, so he couldn't see the man's features. Or woman's come to that. And the thick leathers made the courier look androgynous.

He took the box, which seemed surprisingly light and scribbled his name on the electronic device confirming receipt. The courier melted away into the night and Callum closed the door. Sitting on the stairs he looked at the box. There was nothing written on it, nor taped to it. Not his name or his address. Nor the name of the delivery company, or the company logo of the sender. For the briefest of moments he wondered if he should have accepted the delivery. But he guessed it was too late, as his enquiring nature overrode any disquiet, and he tore the tape off the top of the plain cardboard box.

The moment he opened the flaps and revealed the virtual reality headset inside, he was sold. It looked like something from Star Wars or Star

Trek. He took it reverently out of the box. All black, it had a mirrored surface and two arms, suggesting that you wore it like glasses. The arms weren't hooked at the ends like a pair of glasses, but straight, more reminiscent of designer sunglasses. It certainly wasn't like the style of underwater goggles that other VR headsets used. There was no rubber strap to go around your head and as Callum inspected it, he saw there were no connections, such as USB ports or connections for power leads on it. There were also no hand controllers in the box, so it looked like it connected to a PC somehow.

Callum wondered what game it used, then remembered something being called Penumbra. He scrabbled through the foam chips for a download code but couldn't find one of those either, just a wireless connector for connecting the headset to the laptop. Could the game be in the headset he wondered?

This was way better than he'd ever imagined. It looked as though he would be beta testing a new headset as well as a new game! It was a dream come true for any gamer. He finally found a slip of paper at the bottom of the box. Lifting it out he read the instructions to go to a website and confirm his participation first, before he would be able to start the game. His acceptance also constituted a Non-Disclosure Agreement. Oh my. He wanted to phone his best mate Alex and his hand went to his pocket to take out his phone. Then he remembered the NDA. He couldn't tell anyone. Not even Alex. But even that didn't upset him too much. Let's face it, he couldn't turn down this amazing opportunity.

He turned and ran up the stairs, his fingers itching to start playing.

'Callum,' his mother called after him. 'Where are you going? Dinner's ready.'

'Not hungry, Mum, see you tomorrow,' he replied.

And without so much as a second thought he raced into his bedroom and shut the door behind him.

Chapter 4

On the way home that night, Jo told Eddie about Sasha and Ken.

'That's what I thought would happen, to be honest,' he said, pausing to look either way, checking the traffic, before turning right. 'I could see Ken struggling at times during our last investigation. I can't blame him for wanting to retire now. We'll miss his experience, but he needs to enjoy life while he still can.'

'Talk about enjoying life…'

'Yes?' Eddie said wondering what Jo was up to.

'The family are over tomorrow.'

'Oh,' Eddie's heart sank at the thought of his restful weekend being invaded by Jo's siblings and their wives and children. Not to mention the fact that Honey, the family Labrador, got ridiculously hyper with so many people around and got the zoomies, rushing from one room to the other at breakneck speed. She was guaranteed to make someone trip up, usually when they were carrying drinks or food.

'So…'

Please, please, Eddie silently pleaded.

'I thought we might go out for the day.'

Thanking God for small mercies, Eddie readily agreed. Even a shopping trip would be better than the force that was Jo's family, he knew.

'Let's go along the coast to Portsmouth or

Southampton,' he suggested. 'Give your Mini a run out.'

'Ah, our very own Mini adventure!'

'Exactly,' he said turning into their drive. 'Here we are, home at last.'

Eddie parked his car outside their accommodation. A few weeks ago Mick, Jo's Dad, had offered to let them live in the main house saying he'd take the apartment over the garage. But Eddie didn't feel comfortable with that, so they'd decided to compromise. They would modify the garages under the apartment to make a living room and kitchen downstairs with two bedrooms and two en-suites upstairs. They all tended to share the dog. Or rather Honey was in charge of deciding who to spend time with, turning up unexpectedly whenever she felt like it.

The builders hadn't started the conversion yet, but a firm had been picked, contracts signed, and materials were being ordered. Mick was overseeing the work as he was the one there during the day, being a retired police officer.

Up in the apartment, he found Jo looking in the fridge.

His stomach rumbled. 'Ah good, what's for dinner?'

She quickly shut the door. 'A take away? Delivered?'

Eddie grinned. When Mick started the development, Eddie hoped he wasn't going to choose a huge kitchen full of shiny new appliances that Jo wouldn't use, nor know what to do with. But they had to do something about their diet. Perhaps a cookery course might be in order, for both of them to go on. If they ever got any time off. Perhaps after Jill and Osian's wedding. Eddie lived in hope, as he reached for his phone to order their usual from the Thai restaurant.

Chapter 5

Jo was being led through a forest by Judith, her best friend. Her dead best friend. In the middle of the night.

Suddenly the image changed. She was in a building that appeared to go on forever. The impression was of a long corridor with a forest of doors dotted here and there, some far away, some closer to her, some to her left and some to her right. Large double height windows were glinting in the moonlight. There was something zooming around the ceiling. Jo could feel rather than see it as it passed centimetres from her head. She caught sight of a bat shaped creature silhouetted in the moonlight. Not owls or some other nocturnal animal, but bats.

Jo shuddered. 'I hate bloody bats,' she said.

'Never mind, they won't hurt you,' replied Judith. 'Come on,' and she dragged Jo after her.

'Where are we going? Please tell me,' Jo pleaded. But as usual didn't receive a reply. Still, she was glad to be walking away from the bat. She wondered what else was waiting for her in the darkness. But wondering did no good at all, only quickened her heartbeat and raised her blood pressure. Jo sucked in a deep breath and followed Judith further into the building.

Then Judith stopped.

'In there,' she whispered.

'What is it?' Jo whispered back. Unsure why they were whispering as they were the only people there. Apart from the creatures of the night, they were ut-

terly alone. Then she saw something out of the corner of her eye. A shadowy figure slipping from one of the rooms, out into the corridor. It ran down it, then turned a corner at the end, disappearing from view.

Jo frowned and blinked her eyes. Had she actually seen anything? Or was it just her overactive imagination?

Then Judith turned on her torch. The flash of light was too much for her eyes and Jo could see nothing. Until she closed them. And there, behind her eyelids, was imprinted a horrifying scene. In the torchlight, she'd seen a young man trying to get something off his face. He was frantically grabbing at it. A black slash of some kind. Jo opened her eyes. Judith's torch was still on the man, who Jo saw had forced his fingers behind a pair of chunky black glasses. He pulled and pulled, until, with a grunt and a tearing, popping, squelching sound, it came away from his face.

Looking at the inside of the thing that had been over his eyes, he went rigid with shock. Then screamed. He lifted his face. His head flicked one way, then the other, blood spraying from the wounds. Then he smelled the air and seemed to catch a whiff of something, or someone. Jo and Judith? He stilled.

'Help me,' he whispered. 'Help me.'

His hands came out in silent supplication, but Jo's attention had been taken by the sight of the young man's face.

Specifically by his eyes.
Or rather lack of them.
They were no longer there but stuck to the inside of

the headset he still held in his hands.

Jo screamed. Judith disappeared.

And screamed. The vision disappeared.

And screamed. Until Byrd woke her.

'Hush, Jo. It was just a bad dream.' He stroked her hair. 'Nothing more than that. Hush now. Hush.' Her screams subsided to hitching sobs as she tried to process what she'd just seen. A boy trying to get something off his face, then losing his eyes. Tearing them out of his face. Was it just a dream? Nothing more?

Eddie snaked his arms around her shaking shoulders, trying to rock the nightmare away. But Jo wasn't sure it would be that easy. She just hoped that what she'd seen wasn't a premonition. If it was, they were in big trouble.

Chapter 6

The next morning Callum had not yet made it downstairs and Saturday breakfast was nearly ready. Sarah didn't ask for much but liked at least one meal at the weekend that they all shared. A cooked breakfast, Callum's favourite, seemed as good an occasion as any. It was their routine and one Sarah wanted to continue, especially as Callum would be off to Cambridge at the end of the summer.

She went to the foot of the stairs and called, 'Callum, breakfast!'

She had hoped that the enticing smell of grilling bacon would have roused him, but it seemed not. She called again, but as that made no difference either, dashed up the stairs and knocked on his door.

Her husband, Tony, came out of their room, already washed and dressed and he grinned at her. 'Good luck with that,' he called as he made his way downstairs.

Wishing her husband was more pro-active where Callum was concerned, Sarah rapped once more, then opened his bedroom door. 'Come on, Callum, breakfast.'

Her son was slumped in his gaming chair and it looked for all the world as though he'd fallen asleep playing his game. The laptop screen was blinking 'YOU'RE DEAD' over and over. Shaking her head and trying not to grin, determined to keep up the charade of annoyed mum, she moved to his chair intent on touching him on the shoulder to wake him up.

On his head was something she'd never seen before, a wrap around headset and she wondered if that was what had arrived yesterday. As she touched Callum and called his name, instead of waking up, he toppled forwards, head banging on his desk and only narrowly missing his keyboard. There was still no response from him and a frisson of fear pierced her happy mood.

Shouting, 'Callum!' still didn't rouse her son, so she shouted for her husband. He must have heard the urgency in her voice as he bounded up the stairs straight away.

'Sarah? What's wrong?'

'It's Callum. Call an ambulance! There's something wrong with him!'

As though in slow motion she watched her husband touching Callum's exposed neck and then grab a wrist.

Eyes filling with tears he croaked, 'He's dead, Sarah. Dead.'

'No, no, no NOOOO' she screamed, the call of a wild animal finding its cub dead. Collapsing on the floor she howled and screamed for a son she would never see grow into the fine young man he had been destined to be. All Callum had ever wanted was to learn to develop computer games, but it seemed he'd died trying.

Chapter 7

Jo and Eddie were getting ready for their day out. Not just a good excuse to stay away from her manic family, it was also a chance for them to spend a day together, to be a normal couple. Days such as this were precious and rare, as being police officers involved pretty much being on duty 24/7. It was a life she loved, but just occasionally she'd like for them to be like the rest of the population.

Jo walked from the bedroom and collected a large tote bag from the settee. Never normally one to use a handbag, especially when on duty, today was different. She emptied out the contents onto the coffee table, checking she had her purse and most importantly her credit card. It wasn't often she looked forward to a shopping trip, but Gunwharf Quays with its outlet shops and amazing setting was an exception. Plus the sun was shining, and she was especially keen on lunch overlooking the waters of the Solent, a strait that separates the Isle of Wight from Great Britain. Putting everything back in her bag she'd just called for Eddie when her mobile rang. It was the Chief Superintendent.

'Jo, I know you're off duty this weekend...'

'But?' Jo's heart sank as she could see her day out slipping through her fingers like the body of water she'd been so looking forward to sitting next to.

'But I've got a strange one here,' he said. 'A young man playing a computer game has been found dead in front of his computer.'

Jo frowned. 'Why us, boss?'

'Because he's wearing a type of gaming headset and was testing a new game. It could get complicated.'

Her interest piqued she said, 'Give me the address, sir. Byrd and I are on it.'

Deciding to still take the Mini, Jo drove, as her and Eddie made the journey to Worthing, which was in the opposite direction to Gunwharf Quays. Jo looked in her rear-view mirror as she drove, as though she could see the Solent and her day out disappearing into the distance.

Eddie must have picked up on her introspection as he said, 'You okay, Jo?'

'What? Yes, sorry, miles away there for a minute.'

'You don't say,' he grinned. 'Sorry about today.'

She smiled. 'It's not your fault, but thanks anyway.'

'Another time perhaps?'

'I'll hold you to that,' she smiled in gratitude. 'Maybe after this case?'

'It's a date.'

'So, what do we know so far?'

Eddie activated his phone and pulled up a report from the responding officers that the Chief Supt had sent over for them. 'Callum Walshe, aged

18, found dead in front of his computer screen by his mother this morning. Last seen around 8pm the night before when he took delivery of a package. His father believes that in it was a new headset and game that he had been asked to test. He'd gained a place at Cambridge to do Computer Studies in October, depending upon his exam results.'

Jo whistled. 'Bright boy.'

Eddie nodded. 'He'd wanted to develop video games and had been trying to set himself up as a games beta tester.'

The satnav interrupted Eddie and told them which exit to take on one of the large roundabouts that peppered the A27 from Chichester to Worthing.

Once Jo had made the turn, Eddie continued, 'The parents are understandably devastated as Callum had his whole life ahead of him.'

'What do you reckon?' Jo asked Eddie.

'Let's see what we find at the scene,' he replied. 'But it seems a particularly senseless death.'

'Maybe it's just one of those cases of young men having heart attacks for no apparent reason. Or whilst exercising. Remember those footballers?'

'Oh yes, one collapsed during a Premier League match and another whilst playing for his country. But they were running around a football field. Callum was sat in his chair. Mind you, it can get pretty stressful playing computer games.'

'Really?' Jo said in disbelief.

'Oh yes, you'd be surprised how involved you

get. Especially if it's a matter of life or death.'

Jo looked sideways at him. 'Well whatever Callum was playing, it seems it really was a matter of life or death for him this time, and not just for his character.'

Chapter 8

On the outskirts of Worthing, they easily found the house they were looking for, as it was right on the A27. As Jo turned off the road that could get more congested than the M25, she stopped outside a large house with wrought iron gates to the front, that had been left open. Parked along the tarmac drive, Jo could see two police cars, the forensics' van and two other cars. She pulled up across the front of the house so as not to block anyone in. As she climbed out of the car she looked up at the house. To be honest, she thought the frontage was rather non-descript. The bricks had been plastered over with a textured finish, not quite pebbledash, but something equally as grey and unappealing. There were two large windows on the ground floor and two on the first, but no front door.

'Door's down the side,' Eddie said and she nodded, locking the car and following him.

The door to the house was open, but the way barred by an officer with a clipboard. Identifying themselves and signing in, they were allowed access. 'Parents are to your left, Ma'am, in one of those large kitchen diner family room thingies that are so popular today,' he said.

A door from the substantial hallway opened into an ultra-modern kitchen area, gleaming with chrome and gadgets that Jo had no idea as to their use. She just didn't do kitchens. There was more to life than slaving over a hot hob. Stood looking out of the large bi-fold doors was a man in grey sweats. He turned as he heard them. Jo had the impression of sandy hair falling into his eyes, lightly tanned skin, and toned body.

'Good morning, sir,' said Eddie and introduced them. Then he asked, 'Mr Walshe, I presume?'

The man nodded and introduced his wife who was sat on the settee, also staring out at the garden. As Mrs Walshe turned to look at them, Jo could see blond coiffured hair framing her face. But her features were ravaged by grief. With red eyes and nose, lips pursed, sunken cheeks, she looked what she was - a mother who had just lost her only child.

'Mr and Mrs Walshe, we're so sorry for your loss,' said Jo. 'We'd like to go up and see Callum, but before that, can you tell us what happened?'

Eddie pulled out his notebook as Mrs Walshe turned her head back to the garden. Mr Walshe began to haltingly explain that last evening Callum had received a parcel. 'He'd seemed very excited,' he recalled, 'and ran back up to his room instead of eating dinner with us. I checked in on him before we went to bed and he was engrossed in one of his computer games.'

'Do you know which one?' Eddie asked.

'No, sorry, there was nothing on the screen. Just a black background with the sliver of a new moon showing.'

'That's strange,' said Byrd. 'You normally play with the action showing on your computer screen. What was different this time?'

'The headset.'

'Headset? What, headphones with a microphone?'

'No, this was more futuristic. More like wraparound sunglasses. Callum was manipulating the keys on his laptop and was totally engrossed, so I left him to it. I knew better than to try and get him to stop playing.'

'Yesterday was his last day at school,' Mrs Walshe said, tearing her gaze from the garden. 'It wasn't supposed to be his last day alive. He was going to Cambridge, you know.'

'A bright boy,' Jo said.

'He was only 18! Only 18!' cried Mrs Walshe.

'With his whole life before him,' said Mr Walshe. Then he crumbled. He began to sob. His shoulders shook and he looked every one of his middle-aged years. As he swayed, dangerously close to collapse, Eddie sprang forward and caught him, before guiding him to the settee and his wife.

Jo and Eddie mumbled their condolences, then left Mr and Mrs Walshe alone. One at each end of the settee. Both wrapped in their own personal grief. An ocean of tears between them.

Upstairs, Jo and Eddie were pleased to have arrived before the body had been disturbed. Forensics had swept the room, but the pathologist hadn't yet completed his examination.

'I've got a very bad feeling about this,' Jo said before they entered the room. 'A very bad feeling.'

Eddie looked at her and frowned. 'Any particular reason?'

'My nightmare last night. It might have been a premonition.'

'Well, there's no point skulking out here on the landing, come on, let's go and find out.'

The room emptied and as Jo walked into the bedroom and saw the body, she wondered at the poor boy's fate. He was so young. From what they could see of him, Callum appeared to be tall, muscular and with a shock of sandy hair that matched his father's. Jo was determined to do her best for him. She'd managed to get justice for 10 young men in her last case, so she was sure she could manage it for poor Callum.

Speaking to his parents had been particularly heart breaking. They simply hadn't understood how it could have happened. His mother had kept saying, 'But he was only 18!' over and over again, as though his young age was a talisman that should have kept him safe. But that had failed Callum, and his mother simply couldn't process what had happened. It was the shock, Jo acknowledged.

The sleek black gadget Tom Walshe had told them about, was still on Callum's head, covering his eyes.

It looked too much like the headset in Jo's nightmare than was comfortable, and she didn't like looking at it. She could still see in her mind's eye the young man pulling the headset off himself and his eyes going with it, sticking to the inside of it. Nothing left apart from bloody holes where his eyes should have been.

'Looks like some kind of virtual reality headset,' said Eddie, interrupting her introspection.

She shuddered, then squared her shoulders and took a deep breath. Eddie walked around the desk, looking at Callum from both sides. The bedroom was large, which meant it could accommodate the spacious, bespoke, curved desk fitted into the corner of the room, with plenty of room to walk around it.

'Meaning?'

'You are really immersed in the game. All in. His dad thinks he was trying out a new game with it, as it got delivered last night.'

'It looks very sci-fi,' said Jo. 'That's the best way I can describe it, as though it was from Star Trek or even X-Men,' she said. Jo took a glove off. 'Shall I?'

'I reckon so,' said Eddie. 'Apart from your nightmare, it could turn out to be our only lead.'

Jo nodded and placed her hand on the back of Callum's exposed neck.

Chapter 9

Jo seemed to fall from a great height and then tumbled onto the ground, rolling as she landed, to try and break her fall and not her legs. Scrabbling up, she brushed away dead leaves and twigs from her clothes and looked around. She was in a wood. Fog was licking the tree trunks with gnarled fingers that moved up and down the bark, as though playing a keyboard. The lack of sunlight, which was unable to penetrate both the fog and the canopy of branches above her, further narrowed her field of vision. All was gloomy and menacing. Her hearing was muffled, as though any sound had to travel through wads of padding to be heard.

But despite that, she heard a rustling behind her and whirled around, scanning the trees that were sentries, silent and watchful, brooding and menacing. Nothing. Then soft laughter floated in on the fog from the opposite direction. Mocking. Jo turned once more, scanning the fog. Still nothing.

Then her vision pixelated, as though there was a bad internet connection. Some of the tree trunks went out of focus for a moment, breaking up into tiny, monochrome boxes before settling back into their correct order. Leaves moved, as though someone was scuffing through them, kicking up their heels, but there was no one there. Jo tried her best to relax. It was probably a small animal, unseen in the depths of the debris that littered the woodland floor. But still....

She could feel it. The evil in the air. It seemed

all around. She could taste it. Smell it. Sense it. She had the feeling she was being stalked by something or someone, an invisible entity. The emotional disturbance of knowing someone was out there watching, listening, intending to scare or intimidate her, or even hurt her, was dreadful. Especially as Jo believed she was trapped and felt that she couldn't do anything about it. Her heartrate was increasing, and her breath came out in quick spurts, as adrenaline coursed through her body. Was that what had frightened Callum so?

Without warning, fingers trailed down the back of her neck, and Jo screamed.

The next thing she knew she was pulling her hand away from Callum's neck and collapsed into Eddie's arms.

'The game,' she whispered to him. 'I think it was the game that killed him. There's some sort of predator in there.'

Then she fainted.

Chapter 10

Jo was jerked out of her faint by a foul smell. Coughing and spluttering, she said, 'Jesus, Eddie, what's that?' rubbing her nostrils.

He grinned. 'Smelling salts. They worked, didn't they?'

'Well, yes, but it was disgusting. Anyway I never thought of you as the suave gentlemen in a gothic novel, helping poor swooning females.'

'Oh, now you've hurt my feelings!'

Jo grinned, then struggled to get up. Taking a helping hand from Eddie, she rose to her feet, yet kept her hand on his arm to steady herself.

'So, how bad was it in there?'

Jo grimaced. 'Dear God, Eddie, it was terrible. An empty wood. Malevolent. Heavy with the cloak of evil all around. The more I felt trapped, the more I panicked. Then I felt fingers on the back of my neck that scared the bejesus out of me. And a jolt of adrenaline flooded my system.'

'The flight or fight response kicking in.'

'Exactly.' Jo shivered as she remembered.

'If that kept up, the player could be frightened to death.'

She nodded and moved away, not wanting to talk about the game anymore. 'Come on, let's get out of here.'

Before leaving they arranged with the forensic team leader to have the VR headset from Callum's face and his gaming laptop to be taken into evidence and processed as quickly as possible and then passed to Sasha, so she could examine it.

Finally, they went to find Callum's parents to explain what they were taking away with them. His mother had been sent to bed with a tranquiliser from the doctor, so they had a quiet word with Callum's father and obtained his permission to take whatever they and the forensic team wanted.

That night Jo's dreams were invaded by scenes that she believed were from the game Callum had been playing. No matter where she ran or what she did, she couldn't shake off the feeling that something was very wrong in the gaming world and it, whatever or whoever it was, was trying its best to ensure she didn't speak out.

But Jo wasn't the sort to be scared into silence. People who stalk others, through whatever medium, tend to try to bully their targets into silence, so they can continue their harmful and potentially criminal actions.

Well, not on Jo's watch they wouldn't, she vowed.

Chapter 11

The following day she reported to the Chief Superintendent, who was sitting back in his chair reading a file, which was balanced on his rather large stomach, reminiscent of a pregnant woman. He had a pair of braces on over his white shirt to stop his trousers sliding under his stomach. Jo wasn't sure which look was worse. Braces and high-sitting trousers, or low-slung ones under the protrusion of belly. Either way she was glad she'd saved Mick from this common male fate, by getting him a Labrador puppy for his birthday earlier that year. Now her father was toned from walking and tanned from the sun and wind, as he tramped over the South Downs with Honey in all weathers.

Standing in front of the Chief's desk, Jo told him about their visit to the scene yesterday, including details of her vision when she'd touched Callum's neck.

'Right, in that case, here are details of two others.'

Jo sank into a chair without being asked to sit.

'Two others?' she croaked.

'Yes, I'm afraid so, same kind of thing, young players, gaming on their own, testing out a new game, we understand.'

'Oh, this is awful, sir,' she said. 'Young people losing their lives like this.'

'I know, Jo, but I've got my best team on the

case. So don't let me down!'

'Thank you, sir,' Jo was cheered by the compliment, which was such a turnaround from grumpy old Sykes who'd tried his best to trip her up at every turn. 'Mind you, you know this takes the investigation on to a whole other level?' she said cheekily.

He groaned. 'Get out of here, Jo, and take your graveyard humour with you.' But his smiling face meant his words were not said as a criticism.

Jo hurried back to Major Crimes and called the other three members of the team into her office. Once she had told them about the two other deaths, Eddie briefed them on the visit Jo and he made to Callum Walshe's family home. Then they began brainstorming.

The first things Jo wanted to know were, 'Who is the company behind this game? And just as importantly, how did the players get access to it?'

'And where did they hear of it in the first place?' said Eddie.

'Those questions are for you, Sasha,' Jo said.

'So what do we do next, boss?' asked Eddie.

'We go and meet with the parents of two other players who died in similar circumstances. Jill, here are the files,' Jo passed them over. 'Can you look through them to see the similarities and also do a computer search on HOLMES to see if there are any other deaths in this manner.'

'Let's hope not,' Jill said and shivered, as though someone had just walked across her grave, as Jo's grandmother would have said.

'Indeed. And help Sasha. I know you two have worked well together in the past, so Sasha, are you okay with that?'

'Yes, boss, I can make it work.'

Jo nodded. She knew what it would cost Sasha to have to work closely with a colleague and she saw it as real progress in knitting her team together. For Sasha to be able to do that, it meant that she felt valued and accepted in the team. As far as Jo was concerned, Sasha was an integral member of their small band, Jo just needed to know that Sasha knew it and felt the same.

Chapter 12

Jo and Byrd decided to start with the family furthest away. Sam and Lucy Coleman lived near Winchester, another cathedral city, and the county town of Hampshire. Their son, Robert, known affectionately by the family nickname, Bert, had died four weeks ago. He was only 16.

They lived in the village of Owslebury, five miles outside Winchester. Jo and Eddie drove through the village without realising it. Turning around and going back again, they saw that the village was ranged either side of the main road and seemed to consist of a village green, a pub and not much else. It was surrounded by quiet countryside.

'Not a very exciting place to live to a 16-year-old boy,' she said.

'Not unless you like underage drinking and cricket,' agreed Eddie, pulling up outside the property they were looking for, a terraced cottage, well maintained although not particularly visually appealing. If anything it was rather nondescript and looked like something a child would draw. It had three windows, was built from dark coloured stone, with a washed-out black front door. Their knock was answered by an older man, dressed in corduroy trousers and a muted coloured shirt. At first Jo thought that he was Robert's grandfather. It wasn't until he told them that his wife, Lucy, was in the kitchen, that Jo realised her mistake.

They were shown through to the back of the house into a large kitchen/family room that was clearly an extension. A long, well-tended garden stretched into the distance. They found Lucy Coleman at the kettle.

After the introductions she said, 'Can I get you a drink, officers?'

Jo and Eddie declined, and they all sat at the farmhouse-style kitchen table.

'So,' Sam said, pushing his glasses back up his nose, 'Why are the West Sussex police interested in Robert?'

'It has come to our attention that a case we are working on has similarities with your son's,' Jo explained.

Lucy Coleman uttered a small, 'Oh,' and her eyes filled with tears.

Sam covered his wife's hand with his. 'Now, now, Lucy,' he soothed. Turning to Jo he said, 'So another child has died playing a game, I presume?'

'It appears so, I'm afraid, sir,' said Eddie.

'So what do you want with us?'

'Is there anything else that you can remember that could help the investigation.'

Sam Coleman looked sceptical. 'Help? Help how?'

Jo wondered why Lucy Coleman wasn't saying anything. Ignoring Sam, she said to Lucy, 'What was Robert's favourite game, Mrs Coleman?'

'Um, that fighting thing wasn't it, Sam? Resident Evil?'

'That was when he was 12, Lucy.'

'Oh. Sorry.'

'So you don't really know?'

Lucy Coleman shook her dark curls and looked down at the table. Her hands were clasped together on top of it, and Jo could see where the woman had worried at her fingers, the skin around her nails red raw.

'How long would he play games for?'

Lucy Coleman shrugged.

'How often?'

Again, no response.

Sam Coleman sighed and said, 'He would spend hours up there in his bedroom. God knows what he was doing. We asked, of course. But he would never say much. Just kept shtum.'

So Robert and his mother were both pretty uncommunicative. Like mother like son, understandable, especially around a more forceful personality such as Sam Coleman's. A mature father, probably on his second marriage. Older, wiser, knew better. Jo had seen and heard enough and couldn't wait to get out of the toxic atmosphere.

'Thank you for your time,' she said, standing. 'We will, of course, be in touch if there is anything new to report.'

Chapter 13

Mrs Hayley Devon lived in Lymington, a sprawling town on the edge of the New Forest. They managed to get lost in the maze of new developments, springing up like a rash of measles around the outskirts of the town. Row upon row of new houses, identikit homes for 2.4 child families at exorbitant prices. Jo wondered how people afforded to buy their own houses these days. After a few false starts with the sat-nav and with the help of a friendly local, Jo and Eddie found their way to Hayley Devon.

Here there was more activity for a Sunday morning. People were walking dogs and/or children, kids playing on skateboards and scooters and a few of them kicking a football around a grassy area.

Mrs Devon answered their knock, looked at them, then turned and walked away. A small woman, with bare feet, she had blond hair with dark roots, scraped into an untidy ponytail. Chipped nail varnish and clothes that had not seen a washing machine for a while, completed the picture of a mother who had lost her child. As she'd left the door open, Jo and Eddie shrugged at each other and followed her. The hallway had the pungent smell of stale cigarette smoke, heralding the full ashtray in the front room, which was on a small table set to the side of an armchair that Mrs

Devon was curled into. As they sat, she lit a cigarette with shaking fingers and drew smoke deep into her lungs.

'We're very sorry for your loss,' began Eddie. 'And we'd like to talk to you about Charlie, to help us better understand what happened.'

'There's been another one then?'

'Unfortunately, yes.'

Hayley Devon closed her eyes for a moment, then opening them said, 'What do you want to know?'

'What kind of games did Charlie play?'

'Don't know.'

'How long did she play for?'

'Not sure.'

Eddie took over the questioning. 'All evening?'

'Yes.'

'All night?'

'Maybe.'

'All day?'

'Possibly.'

'So you don't really know?'

Jo was afraid the conversation was swiftly becoming an interrogation and stepped in.

'Mrs Devon, is there anything you could think of that could help us try and find out how this happened. How three innocent children have all ended up dead while playing a computer game?'

Mrs Devon shook her head. 'If there was, I'd tell you. But I just don't know. The whole thing doesn't compute. It's like I'm in the middle of a tv mystery and I don't know how to get out.'

'Could we take a look at Charlie's room?'

She nodded. 'Sure, help yourself. It's the one with the closed door.'

Of course it was, Jo thought. Out of sight, out of mind. But that strategy rarely worked. She walked behind Byrd up the stairs. He pushed open the door to a double bedroom with a single bed in it. There were posters of football teams and computer games on the walls and a table covered in teenage detritus. But no laptop or headset. It must have been taken away when Charlie was found. Jo sat on the bed and looked around. It was a typical gamer's room she guessed.

She idly picked up a hairbrush from the bedside table and started turning it over in her hand while she looked around. Byrd was at the table, looking through Charlie's things.

Then he turned to Jo. But he was no longer Byrd. He'd morphed into someone else.

'Charlie?' Jo said.

The figure turned back without speaking.

Jo rose and went to the table. On the surface now was a laptop. Charlie was sat in her chair with a strange headset on, fingers flying over the laptop keys.

Jo put her hand on the back of Charlie's neck.

Charlie's heart was beating so fast and hard, it felt like it was going to explode. Her face was red, but Jo couldn't see her eyes as they were covered by the headset. She watched as Charlie's head flew from side to side. She must be trying to find someone, or see some-

thing, Jo decided. The vision wasn't strong enough for Jo to see the game as well. She could only see Charlie and the external signs of what she was doing in the game.

Then Charlie pushed the laptop away from her, stood and started to pull off the visor. But she couldn't. It was stuck on. The fear she was already feeling went up a few notches. She couldn't understand what was happening. Why she couldn't get out of the game nor take off the headset. Charlie started to rub her left arm. Then the pain moved to Charlie's chest. She slumped in the chair, clutching the left side of her body. The pain intensified and Charlie grimaced with the force of it. Then with a massive bolt of white-hot pain, Charlie pitched forward and her head hit the desk.

Jo yelped in surprise and fear and dropped the hairbrush.

In an instant Byrd was by her side. 'Are you okay?' He took her cold hands and rubbed them to try and get them warmed up.

Jo nodded. 'Yes, I'm fine.'

But she wasn't fine, she was shivering with cold and fear.

'It was horrible, Byrd. The game seemed so frightening. I couldn't see the game, only Charlie and her reactions to it.'

'Was it the game that triggered the heart attack?'

'It certainly led up to it, but I think it was not being able to get the visor off her face that really caused it.'

Jo's mind flicked back to her nightmare. Then she shook her head, that was the last thing she wanted to think about now. 'Come on, we best say our goodbyes to Mrs Devon.'

Once downstairs, Jo pressed a business card into Hayley's hand.

'If you do think of anything?'

She nodded and Jo and Eddie quietly left the house, as Mrs Devon continued to sit in her armchair and stare out of the window.

As they drove back to Chichester, Jo and Eddie wondered at the lack of parental guidance and knowledge when it came to gaming. The parents didn't seem to have any idea of what their kids were doing. What games they were playing. The horror and carnage they were being exposed to. And for how long and how often they would play. They knew nothing.

'Is it because they don't understand gaming?' Jo wondered.

'No,' said Eddie. 'The parents didn't understand their children.'

'But the kids were all over 16.'

'Only just, some of them.'

'Well, yes, but they should be responsible at that age.'

'The only thing kids of that age are responsible for is getting their mum to clear up after them. Honestly, Jo, they can be very devious, hiding things until it becomes second nature. They won't tell even if it's not that big of a secret. They just do. They become uncommunicative and morose if they're not interested enough in life on the outside.'

'Outside? You make it sound like a prison.'

'Yes, well, their bedroom is a kind of prison, I suppose. It's their safety net from the big bad world outside their bedroom, basically.'

Jo sighed. She didn't understand. But when she was younger, she'd been obsessed by all things horse, she had to admit. She wasn't interested in anything outside the stables and the horses. So maybe that wasn't so different to the kids playing computer games today. Hers was just an outside pursuit instead of an indoor one.

'Maybe there will be some sort of clue from the PM tomorrow,' she said to Eddie.

'We can only hope,' he replied. 'But I wouldn't hold your breath.'

Chapter 14

Strike pushed her way into the computer shop in Littlehampton. Outside the shadows were lengthening into night and inside wasn't much brighter. Her long brown hair was pulled back into a messy twist, while a wide hairband kept any whisps off her face. Her tee-shirt and combat trousers, complete with boots, gave her a no-nonsense look. She could see Penumbra working at a bench that ranged along the back wall of the shop.

'What the fuck do you want?' growled Penumbra without turning to look at her.

'You called for me, dickhead, or are you losing your memory as well as your mind?'

'Cheeky cow.' He turned and leered at her, taking her in from tip to toe.

The close scrutiny made Strike uncomfortable, but she'd never show it. She'd do what she always did in difficult situations, brazen it out.

'Stop being a loser, and get on with it,' she insisted. 'What do you want?'

'Oh, very well,' Penumbra said as he climbed off his stool and sauntered over to her. Handing her a piece of paper he said, 'These are the changes I need making.'

Strike was hoping for a short list, but no such luck. 'Fucking hell, Penumbra, this is going to take ages. Are they absolutely necessary?' She squared up to him. Shoulders back. Spine straight.

But she'd gone too far. Her friend was changing. Normally short in stature he began to grow taller, his body taking on a shadowy quality and he loomed over her. His voice seemed to deepen, as he said, 'If I say I need changes to the game, then I need changes to the game. Yours is not to reason why. Or would you rather face the consequences of not doing your job?'

Strike sucked in a deep breath and with clenched fists drove her fingernails into her hands in the hope that the pain would take her mind off whatever rash come-back she was liable to make. She hated it when he got like this. Bloody computer engineers were all the same, full of their own self-importance. The fact that Strike had coded most of his precious game, was irrelevant to Penumbra. It was his game. His rules.

'It's all right. Keep your hair on. I'll do it.'

After a moment's pause, while he seemed to feed off her fear, Penumbra returned to his normal diminutive self. 'See that you do. And quickly mind.'

Strike turned away. What a dickhead, she thought. But she was secretly glad to push through the door and escape outside, into the fresh air.

Chapter 15

The next morning, Jo and Eddie greeted the pathologist, Jeremy Grogan, at the mortuary in Chichester hospital. He had just begun Callum's autopsy and was doing his initial visual check of the body.

'Young man of 18 years old. Appears well nourished.'

Jeremy began peering closely at Callum's hands. Then he got a magnifying glass and studied the palms.

'What's with his hands?' asked Jo. 'You're playing particular attention to them.'

'Well, kids of this age who mostly play computer games, tend to have problems with their hands and thumbs in particular, a repetitive strain injury. They can also be dehydrated and malnourished from prolonged playing over several hours at a time.'

'That doesn't sound good.'

'It isn't.'

'What about Callum?'

'I'd anticipated all of the above, but it's just not true. He was well nourished, so clearly had a balanced diet. No visual sign of illness or disease. His hands and joints seem fine. I'd guess if nothing else he kept himself hydrated. Anyway, to continue...'

It was 45 minutes later, and after Jeremy had done his internal inspection, that Jo felt she could talk again.

'So, Doc, what killed him?'

'I reckon his heart just stopped.'

'A heart attack? Undiscovered heart disease?'

'No sign of any problems with the heart.' Grogan picked the organ up and inspected it once more, paying particular attention to the arteries and veins.

'Then what happened to him?'

'I reckon he was scared to death.' Jeremy took his safety glasses off and looked at Jo and Eddie. 'Say a friend jumps out at you when you're turning a corner. Your heart starts pounding, and you gasp. "You scared me to death!" But is it possible to be scared to death? Yes. In fact, any strong emotional reaction can trigger fatal amounts of a chemical, such as adrenaline, in the body. It happens very rarely, but it can happen to anyone. The risk of death from fear or another strong emotion is greater for individuals with pre-existing heart conditions. But people who are perfectly healthy in all other respects can also fall victim. It's because of our automatic response to a strong emotion, such as fear. It starts with our fight-or-flight response, which is the body's physical reaction to a perceived threat. This is characterised by increased heart rate, anxiety, perspiration, and increased blood glucose levels.

'The thing is,' he continued, 'adrenaline and similar chemicals in large doses are toxic to organs such as the heart, the liver, the kidneys and the lungs. Scientists claim that what causes sudden death out of fear in particular, is the chemical damage to the heart. Adrenaline increases the amount of calcium sent to the heart. Thus the organ has trouble slowing down, which can cause ventricular fibrillation. Irregular heartbeats prevent the organ from successfully pumping blood to the body and leads to sudden death unless treated immediately.'

'Jesus,' said Eddie and Jo watched as his face drained of colour.

Jo thought Jeremy's explanation might just clarify what she saw and felt when she touched Callum. It was his bodily responses to fear. There was something in that game, as she had said at the time, unseen but felt.

She turned to Byrd. 'We need to know who the maker of this game is, Eddie.'

'Exactly,' he replied. 'Let's get back and see what Sasha and Jill have for us.'

'I'll send my report over once it's typed up.'

'Thanks, Doc,' Jo called as they left the mortuary to return to the office.

Chapter 16

Strike pushed her way into the small computer shop. She leaned against the counter and called to the man she had come to see. 'Oy, Fielding.'

He was in the back of the workshop fiddling with something or other. Strike saw a flash of black as he put down the thing in his hands and sauntered over. He really was one of the strangest men Strike had ever seen. Most of his hair was shaved off, but he was left with a long black tuft of hair falling from the top of his skull. Most of the time that flopped over his forehead into his eyes and he constantly pushed it away. His arms and chest were covered in intricate designs and he wore sleeveless vests so everyone could see them. He was short for a man, five foot and not very much more, but his muscular physique and disturbing tattoos stopped people taking the piss out of his height.

'So I've coded those upgrades you wanted.'

Fielding nodded. 'Nice one.'

'So payment would be good.' Strike squared up to him. You couldn't be a pussy around Fielding, you had to be determined and refuse to back down, or at least those were the tactics she found usually worked best when dealing with him.

'Alright, calm down,' he said and sauntered back to his workbench, where he pulled an open laptop to him. After a few keys had been hit and the screen had been peered at, Strike got a notification on her mobile.

Pulling it out of her pocket and looking at the screen she read it. Payment had been made.

'Don't make me come looking for my money next time,' she said, hoping she sounded as pissed off as she felt. But Fielding ignored her. He'd already turned back to whatever the hell he was working on, on his bench.

Strike battled to get hold of her temper. Bloody man, she fumed. She hated him. But he paid well, there was no denying that. Coding computer games wasn't an easy gig to get into. Unless you happened to be the brightest of the bright, snapped up by the large corporates straight from university. Personally, she'd never fitted into that category. Not because she wasn't skilled enough. But because she just didn't have the personality for the corporate gig. Couldn't think of anything worse than being chained to a desk, coding all day, every day. She'd lose her shit.

She checked the time on her phone and realising how long she'd been away, hurried back to Chichester, hopefully before anyone noticed she'd gone.

Chapter 17

When Jo and Byrd returned to the office, Sasha was nowhere to be seen.

'Where's Sasha?' asked Eddie.

'She went out about 30 minutes ago, but I don't think she's back yet.'

Eddie nodded, but Jo was mildly perturbed. It was uncharacteristic of Sasha. 'Did she say where she was going?'

'No, sorry, boss. And I've no idea where she might be.'

'Alright. So, Jill, what have you got for us?'

'I've been sitting with Sasha as she trawled the deep web and we came across a brief mention of a development company that it is possible are behind the game.'

Jo was relieved. 'A lead at last,' she said.

Jill nodded her agreement. 'I've managed to come up with address details from Companies House but I'm not sure if they are still there. And I've not had chance to check.'

'Don't worry about that, Eddie and I can take it from here. Good work, Jill.'

Sasha was still not back by the time Jo and Eddie left to go to find Dynamic Developments, who could possibly be linked to the new game. They followed the one-way system around Chichester to an area diametrically opposite the police station. On the edge of the pedestrian city centre was a row of terraced houses in a terrible state. Windows were broken and wooden frames rotting. From the street level they could see holes in the roofs. Front doors were missing and replaced by wooden boarding that had been decorated by graffiti tags and badly drawn pornographic images. At the end of the row was a café that appeared to be still open.

Eddie pushed through the door and then held it open for Jo. They sat at a table with chipped Formica on its top, on uncomfortable chairs and was approached by a laconic waitress, who didn't speak, merely stood there until they got the hint.

'Two coffees please.'

'Black or white?'

'White.'

As the girl took her time writing their order in her pad, Jo asked, 'What's happening around here? We saw all the boarded-up buildings.'

The silence continued. Jo thought the girl was chewing gum, or maybe her cheek. She got the impression anything was possible with this one. Piercings sprouted from every orifice, looking more like instruments of torture than decoration. Her black hair was platted, one on either side of her head.

Jo and Eddie showed their identification in the hope of encouraging her to speak.

It appeared to work as she said, 'Oh. Right,' appearing to have found her voice. 'Well due for demolition, innit. This whole block is.'

Jo looked around and decided that any new development had to be better than the quietly rotting buildings and that included the tatty café they were sat in. She seriously wondered how clean the café was and if the front was anything to go by, the kitchen was most likely to be just as bad. The thought made Jo shudder.

'Any idea what happened to the gaming company who had offices down here?'

'Nah, sorry. But Charlie might. He's out back. Hang on I'll get him for you.'

Just as the waitress delivered their coffees, out waddled a man who looked like he'd eaten one too many of his own fried breakfasts. Stale fat smells clung to him, mixed with particularly pungent body odour. His fingers were as big as sausages, his cheeks suffused red with splodges of white on them that made Jo think of Black Pudding, making her glad they'd only ordered coffee and not availed themselves of the all-day breakfast in various permutations that the café offered on garish posters pasted onto the walls. Even their drinks seemed to have come with a sheen of fat over them. She pushed it away. Jo might not be much of a cook, but she had more respect for her body than the owner of the café appeared to have for his own, or even for that of his customers. The idea of looking at your body as a temple, was clearly an anathema here.

In answer to Eddie's questioning, Charlie said,

'Yeah I remember the developer boys. I have no idea what their company did, it was all a bit beyond me, but my nephew seemed excited when I'd mentioned their name to him. Apparently Dynamic Developments are well known in certain circles.'

'Certain circles?' asked Jo.

'Yes, something to do with an illegal web thingy.'

'So where did they go?' asked Eddie.

'Oh, yes, sorry, I told them about an old warehouse building that was being revamped and there were spaces going cheap. Down on the industrial road.'

'Thanks,' said Jo. 'We appreciate your help.'

Jo and Eddie stood to leave.

'What about your coffees?' Charlie called. 'Do you want me to put them in take away cups?'

'No you're alright, thanks,' replied Jo rushing through the door and out into the welcome fresh air.

Chapter 18

Masher sat at his desk staring at his laptop screen, deep in thought. Which was an unusual occupation for him. He was looking at an application form for beta gaming testers open on his laptop screen. He was trying to decide if it was something he wanted to do. Because, if he were honest, a few of the requirements concerned him.

- Strong attention to detail and patience for repetitive work
- Flexible working and the ability to adapt to different processes
- Persistence and perseverance
- Strong computer literacy skills

After all, he was called Masher for a reason. It referred to his repetitive 'mashing' of the buttons on the games controllers in the hope of executing attacks and other various motions found in video games. So basically it could be said that he used brute force and luck to win, rather than finesse and strategy. Ergo he didn't have a lot of patience and couldn't adapt to different processes particularly well.

But then again, there wasn't much to do these days. He had no money so he couldn't go out. School had ended so he didn't see his mates very much. Mum and Dad both worked so they weren't there, and let's face it even if they were, they'd be more interested in the telly and alcohol, than him.

He mentally checked the games he had. He'd completed them all, sometimes twice, with his combination of rapid pressing of buttons and a whole lot of luck. So there wasn't much to interest him there. He toyed with the idea of getting a temporary job, which was immediately dismissed. He was too lazy and hated authority, which was why he always got fired on the first day of his employment and regularly failed his exams at school.

He pushed his greasy hair out of his face, the tendrils of which had been sticking to his acne. He should go and have a shower as he couldn't remember the last time he'd even had a wash. Pushing himself out of his chair he walked over to the window and opened it a crack. He turned and looked around the room at the mess of clothes, dirty mugs, plates, and food containers. Depression wrapped its arms around him. His only companion. Masher had nothing to do, nowhere to go and a pigsty of a bedroom. And most importantly, nothing to look forward to.

Oh fuck it. Nothing ventured, nothing gained, he decided and pressed 'Enter' to send in his application.

Chapter 19

Before Jo and Eddie could go and investigate the warehouses, they got a message from Jill that Sasha was in the office and wanted to update them. So, instead, they made their way back. On their arrival, Sasha was sat at her desk, fingers flying over the keyboard, keeping an eye on multiple monitors. Jo still had no idea what the girl did or how she found the information Jo needed. If she were honest Jo shied away from awkward questions like that and hoped that Sasha's methods never came under close scrutiny.

'Ah, Sasha, at last,' said Jo, unable to stop her irritation showing.

But it clearly had no impact on Sasha whatsoever. She didn't look ashamed, embarrassed, or contrite. Sasha simply acted as though Jo hadn't spoken.

'So,' she began. 'I managed to find an advert for beta-gamers, and I've got a pretty good idea of who's behind it.'

'How did you manage that?' asked Jo, not really wanting to know in case Sasha's methods were not so much illegal, as on the wrong side of legal.

'I found the information on the deep web by giving myself a false username and credentials.'

Jo closed her eyes. The words deep web and false username immediately conjured up illegal activity. 'Won't you be traced back here?'

Sasha laughed. 'Not a chance, boss. I routed through an IP identity cloaker.'

'Are they good then?' asked Byrd.

'Not so much the ones you can normally pick up or buy. I've developed my own by making a few adjustments.'

'Thank you, Sasha, but I don't need to know about any potential illegal activities used to track down the people behind the game. We need to be careful,' Jo intoned.

'But we can't be careful AND find out what we need to know.'

'Are you sure?'

'Positive.'

Jo sighed. She wasn't keen, but she had to trust Sasha who had far more experience in these matters than any of them. Let's face it, she thought, the strange methods and tools she used were no different to Jo's in so much as they achieved her objective. Maybe it was a case of people in glass houses…

Sasha was still speaking so Jo tuned back in.

'Look these things are notoriously difficult to check and to trace, so I have to use any and all tools at my disposal.'

Eddie looked at Jo. 'She's got a point, boss.'

'I suppose so. Oh well let's play that side of things down if it comes to it. Alright?'

They all agreed with Jo. 'Come on then, Sasha, let's have it. What have you found out?'

'This is what I think is going on. Dynamic Developments are trialling a new game. At the moment it's just called WASP324X.'

'What the hell does that mean?'

'No idea, boss. Probably just some letters and numbers that mean something to DD. As far as I can tell nowhere is there a name given to the game.'

'So does that mean it's new?'

Sasha nodded. 'I'd say very new to the market. In fact it could be unlike anything anyone has ever seen before. A real game changer!' Sasha beamed at them.

Jo and Eddie look at each other, bemused. It was unusual for Sasha to be so enthusiastic about, well anything, really.

'Here's a copy of their shout out for beta testers,' and Sasha handed round photocopied sheets.

Are you an experienced gamer?
Why not turn your love of gaming
into a revenue stream?
How?
By being a gaming beta-tester.
You will need persistence and perseverance.
It's not for everyone - only the bravest
and the best need apply.
Can YOU beat Penumbra?

'Penumbra?' asked Jo. 'Anyone any idea what that means?'

'According to Wikipedia,' said Jill, 'the penumbra (from the Latin paene "almost, nearly") is the region in which only a portion of the light source is obscured by the occluding body. An observer in the penumbra experiences a partial eclipse.'

'That doesn't help,' said Eddie and Jo had to agree.

'Perhaps this is better - the penumbra is a half-shadow that occurs when a light source is only partly covered by an object—for example, when the Moon obscures part of the Sun's disk.'

'That makes more sense,' said Eddie. 'A half shadow. In a game it could be a character only half seen. A shadow that you're not sure is there at all, but you keep catching sight of it out of the corner of your eye.'

'Listen to you,' said Jo, impressed. 'I didn't know you knew anything about gaming.'

Byrd half smiled. 'Part of my mis-spent youth. Don't tell me you didn't play computer games, Jo?'

'Not me, horses were my thing.'

'Oh, of course. What about you, Jill?'

'Never really understood them, or what people saw in them.'

'Sasha?'

But Sasha had already turned her attention back to her computer and didn't hear Byrd's question.

Jo looked at her watch. 'OK, let's pick this up tomorrow. Byrd and I will go to the industrial area first thing in the morning. It's getting dark and as we've no idea where we're going, it's probably best to search for DD in daylight. So tomorrow, Sasha keep digging and Jill can you check with the families to see if Dynamic Developments, WASP324 or Penumbra mean anything to them. Thanks all.'

Jo retreated to her office to check her emails and her ever-growing in-tray. She still had loads of paperwork to sort out from the missing men case. Thank God for Ken, who was closing the case while he was working his notice. If it wasn't for him, Jo's tray would have reached volcanic proportions.

Chapter 20

Armed with the new information from Sasha, the next morning Jo and Eddie went to try and find Dynamic Developments. They found a four-story brick-built building with a board advertising rental office space. They parked up and climbed out of the car.

The area was part of a regeneration plan for Chichester's industrial quarter and Jo marvelled at the large warehouses undergoing the transformation from ancient to modern. They started with the first building they found, which was built mostly of red brick. A solid, distinctive warehouse, with four floors, which loomed over them. The windows were large and broken up into squares by what looked like lead strips. Jo had to admire the warehouse vibe that was going on and it reminded her of New York loft-style living. The one in front of them housed both offices and residential accommodation. A large banner advertised two and three bedroomed spacious apartments with many original features at an eye watering price, whilst a smaller one advertised ground floor office space.

'Come on then,' said Jo. 'Let's give this a go. Hopefully, there will be a list of tenants somewhere inside.'

In fact there was something better. A concierge, although a rather crumpled one, who was brushing what looked like brick dust from his suit.

Hearing them enter the building he looked up. 'Good morning,' he called out. 'Sorry,' he said, indicating his clothing. 'Emergency maintenance issue. How can I help?'

Once Jo and Byrd had shown their ID, they asked if he knew of a company called Dynamic Developments.

'Doesn't ring a bell,' he said, and Jo's heart sank. 'What do they do?'

'Computer development, games, that sort of thing,' replied Byrd.

'Hang on,' he said and grabbed a sheaf of paper from underneath his desk. Running down the list with his finger, he stopped towards the end. 'You could try these. The listing says they are gaming consultants, whatever that means.'

'What's their name?'

'Pen... pen something or other.'

'Penumbra?' asked Jo, crossing her fingers.

'Oh, is that how you pronounce it,' the concierge said. 'Bloody queer name if you ask me. Anyway if that's who you're after, Unit 21. Out of the door, do a left, then left again. There should be a plaque next to the front door.'

'Thanks, we appreciate your help,' said Byrd and followed Jo outside. 'What do you think?' he asked once they were out of earshot.

'It must be the right place.'

'That's what I think too. Let's face it Penumbra

isn't your average name. Come on,' and he led the way around to the back of the building.

As the man had promised, there was a plaque by the door saying, 'Penumbra.'

'Here goes,' said Byrd and knocked on the door. There was no reply.

Jo tried. Same result. 'Oh for God's sake,' she grumbled and grasped the handle. Turning it, the door unexpectedly opened, and they walked cautiously through it.

Chapter 21

Two lanky, long haired twenty somethings, both wearing glasses, headphones and gaming gloves that looked suspiciously like supports for their thumbs and wrists, were sat at two open laptops. Not that the laptops were like anything that Jo had seen before. She assumed them to be gaming laptops. She couldn't see what was on the screens from where they were standing. But the machines incorporated large, chunky alphabet keys that were lit in different colours, which changed as Jo watched them. It was quite mesmerising, and she was jolted out of her reverie by one of the young men saying, 'Oh, hello.'

'Hello,' said Eddie. 'DS Byrd and DI Walshe. Chichester police,' and he waived his ID at them.

Did they go pale, or was it just their natural sallow complexion, Jo wondered. After all gamers spent most of their time in the dark – although that was what she surmised rather than knew. She had no experience of games or gamers.

'We want to talk to you about a game.'

'Which one?'

'WASP324X.'

'Okay,' said one of them. 'I'm Rob Downs and this is Kevin Dawlish.'

'DD,' said Jo. 'Dynamic Developments, Downs and Dawlish.'

Rob nodded.

'So why Penumbra?'

'Sorry?'

'Penumbra is the name on the plaque outside.'

Rob grinned. 'Oh that. Kev thought it would be intriguing. Working in the shadows and all that.'

Byrd nodded, but didn't comment.

At last Kev had finished making a show of looking the game up. Jo and Eddie shared a look that said they both thought that was a ploy. Rob and Kev would have known precisely what game WASP324X was and why the police were there. After all the deaths had been widely reported in the newspapers, online and on local TV.

'You understand that we are just a company who co-ordinate the testing phase of the game. We don't write it. Don't own it. We just ask for beta testers, collate the results and feed them back to the client.'

'So who are you working for on this game? Who is the owner?'

Kev scribbled on a piece of paper and handed it to Jo. It was just a gabble of letters and numbers.

'What the hell is this?' Jo passed the note to Byrd. She didn't take kindly to anyone toying with her.

'That's all the information we have. It's a username on the deep web. People post jobs and we bid for them. We got this one. That's all we know.'

'How do you get paid?' asked Eddie, hoping for a money trail they could follow.

'Bitcoins.'

'I should have known.'

Chapter 22

Jo was really peed off and banged around the office when they got back to the station. 'Yet another dead end,' she grumbled to Byrd.

'So, let's be positive,' he urged. 'What's the next steps?'

Sometimes Jo hated Byrd, he was so bloody upbeat most of the time. At least he was a good foil for her grumbling, she supposed. But this case was really getting to her. With all the talk of penumbras, she was seeing shadows all over the place. Shadows that contained something evil. Something lurking in them, waiting for her to cross its path. What would happen when it did catch up with her? Jo had no idea. But she was convinced it wouldn't be good. If only they could make some sort of headway in the investigation, that would cheer her up no end.

'Oh, alright,' she grumbled to Byrd, still feeling a bit grumpy. She called Jill over. 'Have you had a chance to touch bases with the dead boy's families?'

'Not yet, I was just about to call them.'

'In that case, Eddie and Jill, get in the car and go to the players' families. See if the names Dynamic Developments, Penumbra or WASP324X mean anything to them. You should also check with any of their friends and see if anyone will help. Sasha, take this username we were given, see if you can set up another fake ID to lure the suspect out into the open.'

Sasha nodded, not being one for words where a gesture will do.

Jo went into her office and turned to her laptop, to try and find some gaming videos. She felt all at sea because she had no idea what everyone was raving about when it came to computer games. She didn't want to play a game, so figured she could at least get the feel for them via video. Then she had a further idea. She should probably watch any videos produced by beta-testers of new games. Then she'd have a feel for not just the game, but the gamers behind the videos.

A quick search highlighted a video channel. Clicking through to the site she found a player called 'Nebula'. That might work, she decided, after all the term related to Penumbra. One being a cloud of dust or a galaxy beyond our solar system and the other a shadow of the moon. She clicked on the first video and settled in to watch.

After an hour or so, she was fed up with watching battles with monsters, dragons, and other evil entities, with players who had an array of weapons in their arsenal. To be honest, she'd decided, one game was pretty much like another. But not all beta-testers were cut from the same cloth. Some were instantly jarring in their tone and language. Others were so flat and monotoned, as to send her to sleep. It was clear not everyone had the analytical skills and melodic voice that was required to make testing videos.

There was, though, one that intrigued her. The player was wearing a headset, which looked like diving goggles. So far so normal.

But the headset they'd collected from Callum didn't look anything like that.

Jo would have to talk to Sasha.

Chapter 23

Collecting Sasha, Jo made her way to the forensic stores in the basement of the building, insisting they took the stairs and not the lift. Once there, the evidence officer pulled out the headset for them. They took it to a table that was empty apart from an angle poise lamp which they shone on the object.

'Right, Sasha, first of all what the hell does this do?

'I'd guess it's a kind of virtual reality headset. It's used for more immersion in a game. A virtual reality headset of this design, I would say, is a very new piece of kit,' Sasha explained. 'No one knows very much about it yet, but that makes it all the more exciting for gamers.'

'Why?'

'They all want to be the first to test it. It's great marketing, testing something that has a veil of secrecy about it. It makes everyone who's anyone want it.'

'Are there any particular types of games that work best for virtual reality?'

'Yes, VR works well with horror games and jump scares.'

'What the hell are those?'

'Well...'

'No wait don't tell me. Let's have that conversation when Jill and Eddie are back.'

Jo stared at the black band that looked like futuristic sunglasses. All this talk of things she didn't understand was making Jo feel old. It was a way of life almost, and one that she knew nothing about. And she wasn't that old! But this gaming stuff… There was a whole new vocabulary, interests, and explanations to take in. It was all a bit much.

She turned to Sasha. Her computer expert was very quiet, but that wasn't unusual. Sasha didn't really do conversations.

'There's three questions we need answered,' said Jo. 'Where is the game - is it in the headset or in the laptop? How does it tap into in the player? And most importantly for us, how can it affect users, both physically and mentally? Once we answer those questions, we might be on our way to making some sense of this investigation.'

Chapter 24

Eddie and Jill burst through the door of Major Crimes, their sudden entry making Jo jump. They were both talking at once and brandishing a large evidence bag.

'You're never going to believe this,' said Jill.

'Look what we've got,' said Eddie triumphantly.

'We struck gold with Lucy Coleman, didn't we, Sarg?'

'I'll say,' replied Eddie.

'Woah,' Jo called. 'One at a time and start from the beginning.'

'Sorry, boss,' said Jill as she peeled off her coat.

'Byrd, let's have it.'

'Well, we went to see the Colemans. Sam was at work, thank goodness as I never really took to him. We were asking Mrs Coleman about Bert's interest in computer games and ran the names by her; Dynamic Developments, Penumbra or WASP324X.'

'She acted as though we were speaking double Dutch,' injected Jill.

'Exactly. But then she said that there may have been something on Bert's computer. I explained we didn't have it but had put in a request to Forensics in her local area for it. She looked at us oddly for a moment, then said she didn't know what we were talking about.'

'So, she told us to wait a moment, didn't she?' Jill looked at Eddie.

'Yes, and then came back holding a box.'

'And?' Jo couldn't see where this was going.

'And the box contained Bert's computer and headset.'

Jo looked at them wide eyed. 'A VR headset?'

'The very same. When Bert died of a suspected heart attack no one thought anything of it. Tom had taken the headset off his son's face when they found him and later boxed up his laptop and headset and put it in the garage as Lucy hadn't wanted to see it ever again.'

'Sam had told her he'd get rid of it, but thankfully he'd never got round to it,' finished Jill.

'Well done you two.' Then Jo paused. 'And Charlie?'

'No such luck there. Hayley Devon had thrown out her daughter's laptop and headset as she never wanted to clap eyes on it again,' she said.

'But she confirmed that the VR headset he was wearing when he died was the same one as in the picture we showed her.'

'So, there we have it,' said Byrd. 'Proof that the other two kids were wearing the same headset and presumably playing the same game. So what have you two been up to? Have you turned up anything of any significance?'

'Don't be so cheeky,' said Jo. 'We've been examining the headset and talking about what the game could involve to scare our players to death.'

'And that is?'

'Jump scares. Sasha tell them.'

'Not everyone likes them,' Sasha began. 'In fact, they have become the bane of many a horror fan's existence. Some gamers think some brands rely on them too heavily, but sometimes, a jump scare can be well designed. Like any good scare, timing is important, as is building up to the moment. You might not be a fan of them, but when they're done well, they can be great. Some games do them particularly well, mixing terrifying, long-extinct monsters with classic staples of the genre, such as item conservation, puzzles, and an atmosphere thick with dread.

'One of the best jump scares ever was when a T-Rex burst through the window in a game and tried to eat the player's character. Usually, it succeeded in finding its snack, though that's mostly because 99% of gamers dropped their controllers out of sheer fright.

'The Exorcist: Legion VR is based on the third movie in the franchise and is just as disturbing as its source material. The sound design is phenomenal, and it does a great job of building tension with its creepy whispers and sounds that seem to come from everywhere. The intensity never lets up and players will be literally on the edge of, or leaping off, their seat in pure terror.'

'And we think that's what this game uses?'

'Pretty effectively as well, don't you think? The kids were scared to death. Literally.'

That last description pretty much described where Jo was now. Not only was she grappling with the kids who had lost their lives, but with the hidden shadow that was constantly haunting her, no matter where she was. When she was in the apartment and Byrd was either not there, or fast asleep, each creak, snuffle and snore would make her heart jump.

Chapter 25

Strike pounded down the empty streets until she came to the computer shop. It was closed, as was expected. But also as expected there was a dim light at the back of the workshop. Following her nose, she found her way round to the back of the building and pounded on Fielding's back door.

Refusing to stop banging until he opened it, worked a treat and when he did open up, she pushed her way inside, forgetting to be frightened of him, in her horror at what he was doing.

'What the fuck, Fielding? What's with the headsets?' she demanded.

'Nothing,' he shrugged. 'They're just headsets.'

'Really? I don't think they are 'just headsets'. I think they're 'just headsets' that are killing kids. I never signed up for that.'

'What do you mean? Killing kids? Are you mad?'

'No, I'm not fucking mad, you're the mad one if you think you can get away with it.'

'Strike, you better sit down and tell me what you know and how the hell you know it.' A gleam came into Fielding's eye. 'Are you filth?' he asked.

'No!' indignation burned in Strike's eyes. 'How could you think such a thing?'

'Alright, alright, calm the fuck down, will you? You best sit down and tell me what I'm supposed to have done.'

Strike perched on a nearby stool, one leg jiggling, showing the depth of her discomfort, as she told Fielding about three dead young people, who had died playing the game she had helped to code and who were still wearing the headset Fielding had designed and built.

'So the doc thinks they were frightened to death. Had heart attacks.'

'In that case it sounds more like it's down to you, Strike. Maybe you shouldn't have made the game so bloody frightening.'

'But that's the thing, Fielding. I only put in a few jump scares. It wasn't that bad. Maybe your VR headsets are just too realistic.'

'Not a bloody chance,' he said. 'I just basically did a 3D headset, you know, on the same principal of those 3D glasses you put on in the cinema to make the movie more real, so the monsters appear to jump out at you.'

Strike was coming down from her indignant anger high and as tiredness threatened to overcome her, she knew she needed to go home. She stood.

'So, if it wasn't me and it wasn't you,' she said, 'who the hell is doing this to our game?'

Chapter 26

Later that night Jo was awakened by heavy breathing, interspersed with the odd sigh. She could feel and hear the presence. It seemed to be coming from the corner opposite the bed. Jo blinked and looked as hard as she could but couldn't make out a shape. It could have been someone lying on the floor or standing pushed into the corner. She didn't know. Not daring to breathe she slowly eased her legs out from under the duvet and put her feet on the cold floor. Cursing the blackout curtains that were blocking out any light from the moon, she tiptoed closer to the corner of the bedroom.

Then an unexpected whine gave her such a scare that she screamed.

Byrd exploded awake, sat up in bed and called, 'Jo, what is it? Are you there? Where the hell are you?'

She could hear him scuffling around on the top of the bedside cabinet. And then the light clicked on, just as the dog leapt up and started barking.

'Bloody hell,' said Jo. 'What on earth is Honey doing here?'

Byrd laughed. 'She was with me in the lounge after you went to bed and when the film finished, she just sort of followed me in here and curled up in her bed in the corner. So I left her there. Sorry I didn't think it would be a problem.'

'Between you, you both scared me half to death. I thought there was someone in the bedroom with us.'

'Someone? Who?'

Jo shook her head.

'Penumbra?'

'Yes, Penumbra,' she said and burst into tears, feeling extremely shaken and very sorry for herself.

The next thing she knew Honey was trying to lick up her tears and Byrd had his arm around her.

'Sorry, but I've been so scared,' she explained. 'Ever since I touched the back of Callum's neck and made a connection, I've been seeing shadows everywhere.'

'This bloody case,' said Byrd. 'Come on, back to bed with you.'

Jo snuggled into Byrd and Honey jumped on the bed and lay over her feet. Jo didn't have the heart to get her off, as her presence was so comforting.

'We'll get there, don't worry,' Byrd murmured into her hair. 'We always do.'

Jo nodded and matching her breathing to Byrd's she fell asleep, cocooned between two members of the family, both of whom were watching over her and keeping her safe.

Chapter 27

The next day at the station, Eddie followed Jo into her office when they arrived. He hung his coat on the stand, revealing a jumper with an integral shirt collar worn over tan chinos.

'Right, boss,' he said, adjusting his jumper. 'There's something I need to talk to you about.'

Jo threw him a sideways look.

'Alright. Jo,' he corrected himself. 'There's something I need to talk to you about.'

Jo smiled. She hated Byrd calling her boss. She could just about live with it at work, but in private it had to be Jo. And in her office with the door shut constituted private.

'Anyway, as I was trying to tell you, I was doing some research into the side effects of virtual reality headsets last night, after you went to bed. Basically, users can suffer from motion sickness, an asthma attack or even a heart attack.'

'As we know all too well,' replied Jo. 'What I don't understand is why on earth parents would let their kids use them?' She shrugged out of her trouser suit jacket and hung it over the back of her chair.

'Because the use of virtual reality in gaming has changed the way children play games. Gaming has become more intense and immersive. Virtual reality technology can change the way education systems work. We know that the use of interactive methods like audio and visual devices has already made learning fun. This is the next step.'

'I feel a but coming...' Jo sat at her desk. The top of it was empty, but the drawers – well they were another matter. Her files and papers were stored in there under lock and key.

'But,' Byrd grinned. 'They are now developing the next generation of virtual reality hardware, where scientists can activate the brain far more easily than the real world would do. If you believe the hype, it seems that they will soon have the ability to turn on the brain's activity without any drugs.'

Jo realised she was sitting there with her mouth open. 'Jesus, Byrd, that sounds like something out of a science fiction film.'

'I know, it's terrifying. Doctors being able to manipulate our brains just by putting headgear on us.' Byrd ran his hand through his hair, as if his scalp was tingling from the thought.

'I remember when it was experimental skull caps. You know, those with electrodes in to monitor brainwaves. So you're telling me that now instead of just monitoring, scientists can control our brains? Is that what happened to our kids, do you think?'

'What? That the VR stimulated their brains, trying to control them. Or at least inserting an extra dimension into the game. But the experience was just too much for them?'

'Yeah. Too intense. I know I'm clutching at

straws here because I don't really understand it all. But what if it's all about a trial of the headsets and not of the game?'

'That would make sense,' nodded Byrd. 'Not that anything does make much sense here. But it's looking more and more like the beta testers were being used as human guineapigs.'

Chapter 28

A few days after sending in his application to be a beta tester, Masher was laconically playing yet another re-run of Resident Evil. He'd played all of them at one time or another, at least those on PlayStation. Survival horror themed games, which mostly involved shooting zombies, were right up Masher's street.

He stopped playing as he was bored and looked around his bedroom. Jesus, he ought to tidy up, he conceded. Sniffing the air, the smell of rotting food, dirty clothes and BO was a potent cocktail and he walked over to the window and threw it open. As fresh air hit his face, he had to acknowledge that his bedroom was no better than a pigsty. Sighing, he made a start. Firstly he slunk down to the kitchen with his dirty, mould infested crockery and ran away before his mum could tell him off. He didn't go so far as to change his bedding, but at least he made the bed, which was a big improvement. Next, the clothes on the floor were consigned to the dirty washing basket and he then had a shower, marvelling at how grey the water sloshing around his feet was.

Padding back to his bedroom with dripping hair and a towel wrapped around his waist, he heard his mother call, 'Masher, parcel for you.'

Parcel? She must be wrong. Standing at the top of the stairs he shouted, 'Are you sure?'

'Oh for goodness sake,' grumbled his mother and appeared at the bottom of the stairs. 'Yes, I'm sure. See, here's your name on the address label. Now come down and get it, I'm off to work. Oh and those filthy cups and plates you put in the kitchen...'

'Yes?'

'They're soaking in hot soapy water. I want them cleaned, dried and put away by the time I get back.'

'Yes, Mum,' said Masher, rolling his eyes. A thank you would have been nice, he thought. Oh well, there was no pleasing parents.

As his mother disappeared out of the front door, Masher padded down the stairs and collected the box. Taking it back to his bedroom he sat looking at it for a moment. It couldn't be, could it? The game to beta test? Surely, he wasn't that lucky?

Shivering from the fresh air coming from the open window, he decided that if he was going to play a game, he'd better get organised. He closed the window and then quickly threw on some clothes. Going back downstairs he grabbed a couple of cans of coke from the fridge and a couple of chocolate bars out of the cupboard. Sugar rush sorted, he huffed his way back up to his bedroom and put his haul on the desk next to his monitor.

Finally, his hands shaking with anticipation, he opened the box.

Chapter 29

'So,' Jo said pacing the Major Crimes office, 'if we're agreed that Callum, Charlie, and Bert died while playing this new game, I'm wondering if there are any other players?'

'We can't find any more that have died in similar circumstances,' said Jill.

'I realise that, but this morning I had a horrible thought. Are there any other kids with the game right now?'

'Sorry?'

'Any other players who received the game from Dynamic Developments, but aren't dead. So we wouldn't know about them.'

'Oh, sorry, boss, you mean that other boys or girls could be in danger, but they won't realise it.'

'Exactly, Jill.'

'So we need the list of the people Dynamic Developments passed to their client,' said Byrd.

Jo nodded in agreement. 'That's right. Because if there are others, then they need to be warned against using the game and advised to hand them into the police.'

'Do you want to go to the media?' asked Byrd.

'God no. We can't risk mad panic, or speculation about big brother controlling thoughts. Let's see if DD will help first, then we can build a strategy from there.'

'Shall I ring them?' offered Jill.

'No, I'd rather we surprised them. When we're in their faces it's easier to see if they are lying.'

'And easier to intimidate them into telling us the truth.'

'Exactly,' said Jo. 'I'm sure the threat of being arrested will help them remember. Come on,' and Jo grabbed her jacket from her office and when Byrd had collected his, they left the station.

Both boys were in the office when Jo and Byrd arrived. Byrd asked them to stop what they were doing and with much huffing and puffing, and rolling of eyes, they complied. Once all the clacking had stopped, Jo outlined their request of Dawlish and Downs. 'We need a list of the people you sent the game and headsets to for beta testing.'

'We didn't.'

'What?'

'We didn't send anything. We just collected names and addresses.'

'And anyway, why do you want them?' Rob Downs looked perplexed.

'Because we have three dead kids so far and we need to contact everyone else and advise them to stop playing the game immediately,' said Byrd.

'And hand the game and equipment into the police,' said Jo pointedly.

Rob shrugged. 'Let me assure you, officers, that Dynamic Developments wish to fully comply with any and all requests from the police. We would give you the list if we could, but we can't.'

'What? Why?' Jo's anger was simmering and threatening to erupt.

'Because of a Non-Disclosure Agreement.'

'And because we don't have the information anymore,' piped up Kevin Dawlish, pushing his limp hair out of his eyes.

'Anymore? What do you mean, anymore?'

'We are under strict instructions to cleanse the data once the details have been passed to the client.'

'And you do?'

'Of course. If we didn't, we wouldn't have a business. DD are known for their discretion.'

'So you won't help us?' said a dumbfounded Jo.

'We can't. Sorry.'

Jo turned on her heel and marched out of the office, with Byrd following.

Once in the car Jo slammed her fist against the steering wheel. 'I've never heard anything like it!'

'I guess the world of gaming, especially using new proprietary technology, is very secretive. The makers of the game can't risk competitors getting hold of it,' said Byrd.

If he was trying to soothe her, it didn't work. 'Well that doesn't help us though, does it? All these bloody secrets and lies are driving me crazy.'

'No, Jo, it doesn't help. We'll have to find another way. Come on, let's get back to the office. There's nothing else we can do here.'

Jo sighed and started the car.

Jill and Sasha were as dumbfounded as Jo and Byrd when they got back to the office and shared their useless visit to Dynamic Developments. Sasha turned away in disgust, back to her computer, but it was Jill who had a suggestion.

'So how do we find them?' Jill said, musing aloud. 'I know - what about applications for the product design. You know trademark, licencing, that sort of stuff. Oh what on earth is it called?'

'I don't know,' said Jo. 'It's not exactly my area of expertise.'

'No, right,' Jill said. 'It's on Dragon's Den.'

'Sorry, we don't watch that,' said Byrd.

'Copyright? No, that's books and stuff isn't it? Patent! That's it! We can check if anyone has taken out a patent on the headsets.'

'Oh, okay, I get you now,' said Jo. 'I seem to recall that you can also register a design as well, you know. Like the logo for the game.'

'What is the logo?' But no one answered Byrd's question.

'Oh, shit, we don't know,' said Jo. 'Perhaps check any logos that are registered with the UK-Design Register under DD or Penumbra,' said Jo. 'Or the EU Intellectual Property Office. You can ask the Intellectual Property Office to do a search for you for a fee. See if they'll do one for us, Jill as an emergency. We need to know if the company has any design logos registered.'

'If DD has any registered,' cautioned Byrd.

'Right,' said Jo, but she wasn't really listening to him. 'Jill, you check the designs journal and the patents journal. It's pretty much a minefield but we might just get lucky.'

'We could do with some of that,' agreed Jill and bent to her task.

Chapter 30

Masher tore open the box and scooped out hundreds of tiny foam balls. Sitting snugly in the middle of them was something black and shiny. Holding his breath, he carefully lifted out a curved black headset that looked like a giant pair of sunglasses. It was a black, reflective band, hinged at either side to form arms. Immediately Masher thought of Cyclops in the X-men series. It looked rather like the visor he wore to keep his laser vision in check. He wondered if his character would have laser beam eyes that he could use to destroy his enemies. Wouldn't that be cool!

He rummaged around in the box but couldn't see or feel anything else. Where was the game? Frustrated, he tipped the box upside down and balls of foam fell out, bouncing around his floor, rolling under his bed, toppling onto the landing outside his room. But no game. No memory stick. Nothing. Clenching his fists Masher tried to rein in his temper. Was this all a con? An elaborate hoax? Surely the game couldn't be contained within the headset. He turned it every which way, but there were no clues there. Not even a button to turn the bloody thing on.

He was just about to throw it across the room when he remembered Cyclops again. Perhaps he needed to put the headset on, to trigger it somehow. Why couldn't people include user information or instructions. Mind you, not that Masher would have read them. Somehow instructions and Masher didn't really get on. He became frustrated with the slowness of it all and started bashing keys and playing around until he got the hang of whatever it was he was trying out. Rather like his dad trying to put together flat pack furniture when he was drunk.

Feeling that the logical thing to do was to put the headset on, he slipped it over his eyes and balanced the arms on his ears.

Immediately a strange logo appeared, to be whisked away and replaced with the name, 'Penumbra.' Underneath that was the words, 'Please wait while we connect you...' Then came the confirmation. 'The headset is now remotely connected to your laptop. Please use the controls on your keyboard to navigate around the game.'

Then the words were replaced with a panoramic view of the opening of the game. Wow, thought Masher. It was awesome. As he moved his head, so the landscape moved with his vision and as his eyes became accustomed to what he was seeing, he realised that he was fully immersed in the game.

'Hey,' he called out. 'I am my character. I feel what he feels. Am doing what he does. This is bloody amazing!'

To begin with, Masher felt overwhelmed, a bit dizzy and sick. It was definitely all a bit much to start with but gradually he got used to it as he navigated Penumbra's world. He heard a voice in the distance, calling his name. It must be his mum, he realised, but he couldn't stop. He had to continue.

He was so immersed in Penumbra's world that he wasn't aware that she'd entered his bedroom, until she touched his shoulder, breaking his concentration.

Wondering what the hell she wanted, he tried to get headset off. He couldn't. It wouldn't come off. It was as though it were stuck to his head. He was stuck in the game. Stuck in Penumbra's world. He realised he had to play the game until the end. It was the only way. It seemed he could only go forwards, not backwards.

But what would happen if his character died? Will he be able to get the headset off then? Or will he die?

What the hell had he got himself into, was his last conscious thought. And then he fell into the game.

Chapter 31

'Sasha have you found the time to look at that headset yet?' asked Jo as she came out of her office.

'Yes,' said Sasha, frowning. 'Of course I have.'

Jo had to bite her lip to stop herself demanding why Sasha hadn't told her that rather important piece of information.

'And what do you think?' quickly interjected Byrd, who must have seen the look of frustration on Jo's face.

'I reckon it's a VISOR.'

'Yes, I think we've gathered that, Sasha,' said Jo, still peeved with the girl.

'No, you don't understand. A VISOR as in Star Trek, not just a covering for the eyes.'

'Oh,' piped up Jill. 'La Forge.'

Sasha nodded.

'You've lost me,' said Jo.

'And me,' said Byrd.

Sasha rolled her eyes but explained. 'The Wikipedia explanation is that in the Star Trek fictional universe, a VISOR is a device used by the blind to artificially provide them with a sense of sight. A thin, curved device worn over the face like a pair of sunglasses, the VISOR scans the electromagnetic spectrum, creating visual input, and transmits it into the brain of the wearer via the optic nerves. There are sensors located on the convex side that covers the eyes and it attaches at small input jacks implanted in the temples. The only VISOR seen on screen was used by Geordi La Forge, who was blind from birth. VISOR is an acronym for "Visual Instrument and Sight Organ Replacement."'

'So, let me get this straight, it gives blind people back their sight.'

'Not exactly. In Star Trek it didn't reproduce normal human vision but did allow the character to "see" energy phenomena. Human vital signs such as heart rate and temperature, giving him the ability to monitor moods and even detect lies in humans.'

'Jesus,' muttered Byrd. 'So is this visor straight out of science fiction too?'

'Yes and no. I think it immerses the player in the game, but what they see is normal human vision. Penumbra is the name and logo that appears when the game starts,' said Sasha. 'It seems to be controlled by the headset, not by the computer. You don't have to load it or download it. There's no stick to put in the computer, there's no trace of it on the computer, just Penumbra registered on the pc as a new device.'

'Talking about registering,' said Jill, 'from what I can gather it's not registered anywhere! Not as a patent nor as a design logo. Sasha gave me a copy of the logo to check the registers with, when she found it.'

'Really? Shit. I was convinced the headset device would be using proprietary software and would in its own right be proprietary hardware. So if that's not the case, where do we go from here? Who the hell built this thing?'

'I've no idea but we have to bloody well find him,' said Byrd.

'Or her.'

'What?'

'Or her.'

'Yes, sorry, Sasha. Or her.'

'Look,' said Jo, glancing at her watch. 'I've got to go and see the boss. Eddie and Jill go back to Dynamic Developments, will you? See what you can get out of them.'

'And lean on them?'

'Absolutely,' agreed Jo.

'Come on then,' said Byrd to Jill. 'I'm going to enjoy this.'

Chapter 32

The two boys from Dynamic Developments looked like they were just leaving when Jill and Byrd turned up. Byrd was quick to make sure they turned right around, went back inside, and answered his questions instead.

Once Jill and Byrd were in the office, Byrd stood in front of the door, blocking the exit. 'Right,' he demanded. 'What can you tell us about Penumbra?'

Byrd watched as the two men went pale, if that was possible. Paler than normal anyhow. They looked like walking skeletons, Byrd decided. All skin and bone, jackets that hung from their shoulders, trainers that made their feet look huge on the end of spindly legs. He was beginning to think that all this computer developing, and gaming, was bad for your health. Or, if you weren't careful, it was a ticket straight to hell.

'Oh, so you've found that out, have you?' said Rob. 'There's nothing to tell, it's just another game.'

Byrd smiled, a sardonic grin with no humour in it. 'Don't play around with me. What haven't you been telling us? How many more youngsters have to die before you help us with our enquiries?'

The men looked at each other and eventually Kev nodded. 'OK, Penumbra contacted us.'

'And who the hell is he or they, was my question.'

'We really don't know.'

'Really? Pull the other one. I'm sure you can do better than that.'

'And we were scared into keeping quiet.'

'How?'

'They threatened our parents.'

'They?'

'We don't know. They, he, she, what's the bloody difference? We were told if we ever breathed a word of this, they would kill our parents and us. Or us and leave our parents in a living hell as they'd make it look like suicide. Or our parents and we'd then be in a living hell, knowing we'd effectively murdered our own mum and dad. Isn't that right?'

Kev turned to Rob for confirmation who nodded enthusiastically. For one brief moment Byrd felt as though he were watching Wayne's World. The bit of the film where the four were nodding enthusiastically to Bohemian Rhapsody. The boys had the same long hair and gaunt features as those in the film.

'And you believed the threats?' asked Jill.

'Of course we bloody did. It's been awful, we feel like we're being watched all the time. It's like having a shadow in the room. We keep looking over our shoulders, catching sight of something or someone out of the corner of our eye.'

'It's been like that ever since we started working for Penumbra. You know?'

The trouble was that Byrd did know. The tension from being stalked by something or someone unknown could be a living hell. Maybe that explained the unkempt appearance of Rob and Kev. Maybe they really were living on their nerves. Afraid of Penumbra. Afraid of their own shadows.

For a moment, Byrd felt cold and pulled his jacket around him. It wasn't a draft exactly, more like he was standing in front of the freezer with the door open. The sensation passed as quickly as it had come, but for a moment it had chilled Byrd to the bone.

'And there's really nothing else you can tell me?'

Byrd hated to kick anyone while they were down, but it was imperative they got a hold over the investigation, become proactive instead of just reactive.

'No, honestly, we've told you everything we know. We really didn't keep records. We followed the rules set out by Penumbra. It was more than our lives were worth not to. Literally.'

Byrd nodded and turned to open the door. He was having cold shivers down the back of his neck. He resisted the impulse to whirl around. He didn't want DD to know that he was affected by the atmosphere in the office as well.

'Thanks,' he managed to mumble to Rob and Kev, then gave in to the desire to get the hell out of there.

When Byrd relayed his conversation with the two men to Jo, she was disappointed at the lack of progress.

'And you believed them?' she asked Byrd.

'Oh yes, I believed them alright. It was as though I could feel something with us in that bloody office. I couldn't see anything, but…'

Byrd seemed to lose focus and the thread of what he was saying. Jo gently prompted him, 'But what, Eddie?'

His eyes met hers. 'I could feel it, you know? There was a malevolence in the air. A malevolence with attitude if you get what I mean. Challenging me. Daring me to go up against it.'

Jo nodded. If she was being honest with herself and with Byrd, she did know exactly what Kev and Rob had been through. Were still going through. What they'd told Byrd had also been her experience ever since she'd touched Callum on the back of his neck. She'd been jumping at shadows and battling with a feeling of impending doom.

'What the hell have all these kids got themselves into?' she said. 'And how the hell are we supposed to stop the force that has been unleashed by the bloody game?'

Chapter 33

The following morning Jed from the front desk called up to Jo's office. 'Guv, there's a strange one here. Isn't that what you lot do? The strange ones?'

Jo smiled, 'Yes, something like that. What have you got?'

'Well, I've just overheard that two young, uniformed policemen were called to a warehouse unit in Chichester on the industrial estate. It seems that two lads there have been, well, badly mutilated is the best way to put it.'

'Any idea who they are?'

'No names yet, but they were found at the office of Dynamic Developments.'

Jo dropped the phone in shock. Scrabbling to pick it up she could hear Jed shouting into the phone, 'Guv? DI Wolfe!'

'Sorry, Jed, I'm here,' she said. 'Must be a bad line or something. Were the two found dead?'

'No, they've just gone off in an ambulance to Chichester General. Forensics are on the scene and DI Logan is the SIO.'

'Perfect, thanks, Jed.'

Jo called for Eddie and as they clattered down the stairs, he said, 'Jo? What on earth's wrong?'

'I'll tell you in the car on the way.'

Once at the hospital Byrd went straight through the 'No Entry' doors into A&E, flashing his badge to anyone that looked their way. Jo decided she'd leave Byrd alone as well, judging by the look on his face. It was as dark as thunder. His chin jutted out, his brow furrowed, and his eyes swept the busy space which was being criss-crossed by staff. Medical staff were dressed in scrubs, porters in dark trousers and jumpers and there was the odd civilian trying to catch the eye of busy nurses.

Finally Byrd found the man he was looking for. 'There he is,' he said to Jo. 'Come on.'

With three strides Eddie stood in front of his friend, Gill, an A&E doctor and his main contact for all things hospital related. 'Gill, thank God I've found you.'

'Eddie! How are you?'

It seemed the doctor soon got the hint from Byrd's silence and the expression on his face and said, 'Ah, not a social call. I take it you're after my two mutilated men.'

'Yes. Can we see them?'

'Briefly, before they go into surgery, come on,' and he led the way to two bays at the end with their curtains closed.

'Are they conscious?' asked Jo.

'Yes, but…'

'Good,' interrupted Byrd. 'We need to interview them as soon as possible.'

'I'm afraid you can't.'

'Look, Gill, don't stand in my way. This relates to a case of murdered teenagers that we're investigating, and we need to speak to these two men urgently. Before they go into surgery.'

'You don't understand, do you?'

Byrd and Jo looked confused.

'Understand what?' said Jo.

'They can't tell you anything. Their eyes have been removed and their tongues cut out.'

Chapter 34

It was the end of yet another exhausting, frustrating day. Jo still couldn't believe what had happened to the boys from Dynamic Developments. The medical staff had confirmed that they couldn't do anymore for the two injured gamers. Their eye sockets had been cleaned out and stitched up and that was just about the best they could do. It was a miracle that they'd not died of blood loss. It was only because someone had pulled the emergency cord system at the office, that they'd been found in time. It seemed that whoever had done this to the two men, hadn't wanted them to die.

DI Logan had sent through his report. When the two had been found, they'd been tied to chairs, mutilated and then their eyes and tongues were left in a jar next to them. There were no leads at all. No fingerprints in the office other than those of the two men. In fact there was no forensic evidence that would point as to who the perpetrator might be. It was as if someone, or something, unreal and unseen had entered the office and hurt them. As DI Logan had put it, it was almost like a locked door mystery.

Wandering into Jo's office, Eddie slumped in a chair and picked up the headset. 'I used to be good at these, you know?'

'What? VR headsets? In your day?'

He laughed, 'No, gaming.'

'Oh, so you were one of those geeks who sat around for days on end playing on your console?'

Byrd ignored the jibe. 'I used to like the new games. The challenge of them. To see how many days it would take me to beat it. Then I'd trade it in for another one.'

'You had a lot of pocket money then?'

'Not really, mum used to help me out, but I was pretty good at finding money to fund my hobby.'

'Obsession.'

'Pardon?'

'These things seem to me to be an obsession.'

'I wonder if I'm still any good? Maybe the only way to stop all of this is to defeat Penumbra?'

Watching in horror, Jo realised what he was about to do. 'Eddie, no! What the hell do you think you're doing?'

But it was no good, she couldn't stop him. He'd already put the headset on.

And he couldn't take it off.

Chapter 35

Jo watched in horror as Eddie turned round her laptop. She saw the Penumbra logo on her machine and watched as he clicked on the icon. Then a welcome screen showed up.

Welcome to Penumbra.
Where things wait in the shadows.
Choose your character.

Someone was speaking the words as well as them appearing on the screen. It was an eerie male voice. Deep, resonant, and vaguely threatening.

Eddie clicked and clacked, then the next message appeared, and the speaker said, 'Overlord, eh? Nice choice. But is he good enough to beat Penumbra?'

Now Jo felt as though she were watching an episode of The Cube. The words, 'For £100,000 can YOU beat the Cube?' played over and over in her head like an annoying case of tinnitus.

Then her laptop screen went black, and very slowly a picture of the sliver of a new moon appeared. Jo was no longer able to see what Eddie could see. He would start playing the game and she would be left outside. Blind. Unable to reach him. Unable to help.

Eddie pulled the laptop closer and started to manipulate the arrows and F keys on her keyboard. She still couldn't see what was going on. She felt as though the sliver of moon was mocking her.

That's when Jo realised, she couldn't get Eddie back. He was lost to her. Lost in the game. She couldn't let him face this alone. There was only one thing she could do.

She reached out and put her hand on the back of his neck…

Chapter 36

That evening Jill was working away at home. She'd decided to start at the beginning of the investigation again and was perusing the case file for anything she might have missed. She was interrupted by Osian arriving for supper.

As she was getting him a glass of wine, he wandered over to the sofa and looked at the file she'd left open on the coffee table. 'A new case?' he asked. 'Anything interesting?'

'Yes, this game Penumbra.'

'Penumbra? Like in the shadow of the moon and all that?'

'Yes, that sort of thing. But kids who are testing it, end up dying.'

'Good heavens.'

'I know, horrifying isn't it?'

Osian took a closer look at something in the file, then said, 'I've seen that design before.'

'What design?'

'The one here, the silhouette of a man with a sliver of the moon in the sky.'

'Really? Where?'

'I'm not sure. It's in there somewhere,' and he tapped his temple. 'Maybe it will come to me. Anyway, did you say something about supper?'

Jill collected her papers together. 'Your wish is my command, Master,' she intoned and they both laughed.

The video game was soon forgotten as they ate and drunk and planned their wedding. It was to be held at the Cathedral, of course, because of Osian's position there. But Jill had wanted a quiet, more intimate gathering, so they had agreed to a small ceremony in the Lady Chapel.

Chapter 37

Within minutes of stepping into the game and trying to get the hang of the controls, and of his character, Overlord, Eddie was drenched in sweat. His heart was going nineteen to the dozen and he couldn't remember being as frightened as he was then. Well, maybe he could, on the couple of occasions when he thought he'd lost Jo to some demon or other. But he had to admit that this time it was worse. He could lose his own life and potentially Jo's, as he could feel her connection to him, with her hand on the back of his neck.

That did the trick, thinking of Jo in there with him. It gave him a modicum of courage to face down the unknown threat that was Penumbra. It's what they did. Worked together. Which operated on so many levels, both privately and professionally. He admired her tenacity, her courage, and her devotion. With her by his side he could do anything. He could be as invincible as Penumbra. He hoped to God she didn't break her connection by going home. But she wouldn't do that. She'd never leave him battling alone. Careful not to get sidetracked, Eddie bent once more to his task.

'E d d i e,' the whisper came to him, floating in the night.

He shook his head. He wouldn't take any notice.

'E d d i e,' this time it was said with a hiss. There

was an urgency in the voice. But Eddie was too nervous of possible tricks to take any notice. He tried to push away the voice, block his mind to it.

'For God's sake, Byrd, it's me! Judith!'

Eddie nearly took his hands from the keyboard in shock.

'What? Judith? Where are you?'

He turned 360 degrees but couldn't see her. There was only shadows and swirling mist.

'Behind you.'

He whirled around. And there she was. Judith. The ghost who'd helped them many times since she'd died in that horrible explosion in the Italian restaurant. She looked the same as Jo said she always did. A little burned and frazzled with whisps of smoke coming from the back of her head. Her usual way of communicating was via a mirror, but this time she was in the game with him, which he wasn't complaining about.

'Judith, is that really you?' Eddie was still very wary.

'Of course. Um, how can I convince you? Let me see. Oh yes, you're in the office, Jo has her hand on the back of your neck. You now live together in the flat over the garage. Jill and Osian are at this moment in Jill's flat discussing their upcoming wedding in Chichester Cathedral in the Lady Chapel. Anything else you'd like to know?'

Eddie could feel tears threatening, as he let go of his fear now that there was someone he could believe in, in there with him. Since when had he become so emotional? Since his life and all he held dear were on the line, he guessed.

He coughed away the lump in his throat. 'Judith, am I glad to see you.'

She smiled. 'I thought you might be. Look I'll stay at your shoulder. I can't do much in the way of hurting Penumbra, but I can help you see where he is. If I catch sight of him, I'll tell you. Is that okay?'

'More than okay, it's good to know you've got my back.'

Eddie had all sorts of questions for Judith but needed to keep his wits about him. His queries would keep until he'd won the game and beaten Penumbra.

Which he WAS going to do.

Wasn't he?

Chapter 38

After a filling supper and a couple of glasses of wine, Osian was feeling happy and fulfilled. He still couldn't believe his luck that someone as wonderful as Jill would be in love with him and what's more, want to be his wife. He'd thought his life was complete when he'd joined the priesthood, but now saw it was only the first step in the journey that the Lord had mapped out for him. Jill was strong, as was her faith. She was intelligent and caring and he was sure she'd make a wonderful clerical wife. Her empathy and compassion for people was growing every day and he likened her to a flower bud opening its petals one by one until all its beauty was revealed.

Then his thoughts turned to Jill's latest case. This one was a little different to their usual investigations. An image of his trembling hands as he got ready to shoot the Kelpie in their last investigation, flashed into his mind and he still shivered at the thought of what might have happened had he missed. Still, he wondered who or what this Penumbra was that the team were chasing. To be honest he sounded as evil as anything they'd faced before, only this time their demon was inside a computer game, waiting to pounce on every unsuspecting player.

As his footsteps rang through the quiet streets, he kept turning over the name in his mind. Penumbra. Penumbra. What was it that was familiar about it? And then he remembered where he'd seen the Penumbra logo that Jill had shown him.

It was a sketch he'd seen on Sasha's notebook when they were in the middle of the investigation of the lost men. He remembered admiring it and was going to ask her about it, but then things escalated, and he never got the chance. To be honest the events on the beach at Pagham had wiped most things from his mind.

He'd have to let Jill know, but as he opened his phone, he realised it was gone 11pm. Poor Jill had looked worn out when he'd left and was going straight to bed. So he figured he'd let her sleep. It would do her good. And anyway the information would wait until the morning.

Chapter 39

No sooner had Eddie got used to Judith being in the game when another player joined them. A beast called Masher suddenly appeared.

'Hey,' Masher said. 'I think we're after the same thing.'

'Penumbra?'

'You bet. Two against one, eh? That's better odds.'

Eddie sighed with relief. Two players, and a half if you counted Judith, against the shadow that was Penumbra was much better odds than when he'd first slipped on the headset.

'Right,' Eddie said to Masher. 'This is what I think we should do...'

He was halfway through his rather lengthy explanation of what weapons they had, how they could best be used, when Masher interrupted. 'Mate, let's just throw everything we've got at him.'

Eddie paused. Well, maybe Masher had a point, he conceded. 'Okay, let's do it.'

All this time Jo had been following Eddie as he played, through the connection she had with him via her hand on his neck. She was doubly encouraged, firstly by the appearance of Judith and secondly that of Masher. She didn't understand computer games, had no idea how to play them.

She kind of figured that Masher's theory was as good as any. Just chuck everything at the baddies. The problem was that they had no idea where Penumbra was. He was still hiding in the shadows, following the players, monitoring their movements. The air of menace in the game hadn't gone away, in fact it had intensified as the two players fought their way through the various levels of the game. She understood enough to know that you had to win each level before you could progress upwards to the final level. She guessed that last one was where they'd meet Penumbra.

Jo was getting tired and thirsty, but she knew she couldn't take her hand off Byrd's neck and break the connection, as she might not get it back. She'd never been so frightened in her life. Ever. Not even when fighting the apparitions from hell.

She was terrified because this time the life on the line was Eddie's. Her soulmate, her love, her everything. If he died, there would be no point in her living anymore.

If she were honest, she'd cried a little when Judith had appeared to help Byrd. Silent tears that rolled down her cheeks, to be dashed away by her free hand. She took strength from Judith's appearance. She had never let them down, and even though Judith was dead, Jo still saw her as an integral part of the team. It was just that she was normally invisible to everyone except Jo. But in Jo's eyes that didn't make her any less real, any less able to help.

Chapter 40

As he and Masher progressed in the game, Eddie could still feel the vibrations from Jo's hand. He loved her more than life itself and he was determined not to die in the game. With Judith and Masher, together they should be able to make it work and if Jo stays with him as well, even if only for moral support, then the more the merrier. Although it wasn't merry at all inside the world that was controlled by Penumbra.

The evil monsters they were fighting had the ability to flit from place to place. One minute they were in front of you, the next behind. To the right. Then to the left. They didn't run, jump, do somersaults. They just appeared and then disappeared in the blink of an eye, with no warning. It was unnerving and very draining. A number of the levels were set in woodland: dark and shadowy, where the portent of danger was strong. Those were the most taxing levels. The trees appeared to whisper to each other, which was a huge distraction. Overlord and Masher would tread carefully through the forest, but then their presence would be detected because of the crack of a twig underfoot, or the rustling of leaves on the forest floor. And then a demon would be there, ready to throw a bolt of lightning or worse, and blow you to kingdom come.

It seemed to be permanently night, as they

were living in the shadow of the moon. Occasionally dawn would start to break, signifying the end of that level. At the beginning of the next level it would be dusk, with the shadows lengthening and the night noises of the beasts in the dark becoming louder and more strident.

The trouble was that fear was always heightened at night. The prospect of not being able to see who your attacker was, or where he was, meant that you were always on your guard. All your senses were working in overdrive. Ears picked up every little noise. Taking shelter behind trees, Eddie could feel the roughness of the bark under his hands. Emotions ran amok and the fight or flight response because of the adrenaline coursing through him, was strong.

It meant the players battled themselves, as well as the invisible foe. Eddie knew he had to stay calm or the chemicals flooding his system would kill him and potentially Masher.

Chapter 41

Jill was eating breakfast when Osian rang the next morning.

'I've remembered where I saw the logo,' he told her.

'Oh well done. Where was that then?'

What Osian said next stopped her in her tracks. She'd had a piece of toast in her hand, halfway to her mouth and it stopped there. Then fell to the plate.

'You saw that logo on a notebook?' she managed, her voice trembling.

'Yes. Sasha's notebook. And when she realised I'd seen it, she quickly turned the notebook over, hiding it from me. I've never seen it since.'

'Sasha? I can't believe this,' said Jill. 'She must have knowledge of the game. Maybe she's played it. Or helped develop it. Or knows who does.' Jill's words came tumbling out, tripping over each other in her haste and shock.

'Is she behind it do you think?' Osian asked. 'This game? Those deaths?'

But Jill was in denial. 'No, surely not. I would know, I work with her every day.'

'Yes,' persisted Osian. 'But how much do you really know about her? Where she lives? Friends? Hobbies?'

'Now you come to mention it…'

'Exactly,' he said, a note of triumph in his voice.

'Osian I have to go. I must tell Jo and Eddie. I'll try and raise them on my way to the office.'

'I'll meet you there.'

'But don't you...?' She knew he had a meeting that morning.

'I'll cancel. This is far more important. You might need help catching this latest demon and I won't let the group down.'

Jill was so relieved. Osian's words brought tears to her eyes. But she couldn't break down yet. There was work to do. Sniffing she grabbed her bag, keys and phone and ran.

Chapter 42

By now Eddie and Masher had teamed up with a further player whose character was called Prince. They'd found him lurking in the shadows, pinned down by a group of three thugs. Masher and Overlord had used their superior fire power to thwart them and free Prince. That meant there were three of them battling together to get to the final level, which eased Eddie's fears somewhat. It would be harder to stop all three of them when they were working together. They'd have a much better chance together than apart.

The mention of the name Prince reminded Byrd of the prince in Sleeping Beauty. He'd had to battle through the maze of thorns to get to the princess and wake her with a kiss. Eddie had to get to the end of the game and defeat Penumbra, so he could kiss Jo again.

Mick was looking out of the window, deciding whether to take Honey for a walk now or later. His musings were interrupted by his mobile ringing.

'Mick? It's Jill from Chichester Police.'

'Hello, Jill. What can I do for you?'

'Look I'm sorry to bother you but I haven't been able to raise Jo or Eddie.'

'That's unusual.'

'I know, so I wondered if you'd seen them.'

'Sorry, love, I haven't. Just hang on,' and Mick

returned to the window.

'No, there's no cars there. Come to think of it, I didn't see their cars last night either. And Honey hadn't barked at their arrival, which she always does, so maybe they stayed somewhere else overnight? Are they still at the office?'

'I don't know. I'm on my way there now.'

'Sorry I can't help you.'

'Not to worry, it's probably just me, worrying over nothing as usual. Thanks. Bye.'

As he placed his mobile back on the table, the call had Mick worried and he snatched it back up again. He tried Jo's mobile and then Eddie's and finally the landline to the flat for good measure, but there was no answer on all three of them. And that was what concerned Mick. Where the hell were they? What had happened to them? Knowing the work they did and the sort of people and things they dealt with, Mick quickly fed Honey, let her out for a wee, then grabbed his car keys and ran.

Chapter 43

Jill parked haphazardly in the police car park and rushed around to the front of the building. She met Mick and Osian on the steps of the police station and together they went in.

Once at the desk she called to Jed, 'Have you seen Jo? I mean DI Wolfe and DS Byrd?''

'No, sorry, love. Not this morning. Mind you I don't recall seeing them leave last night. Knowing those two they could have pulled an all-nighter.'

The three of them rushed up the stairs and Jill stopped at the entrance to Major Crimes. Jo's office was at the far end of the floor and Jill took a moment to take a few deep breaths to calm her nerves.

The three of them approached Jo's office filled with trepidation.

The relief at finding Jo and Eddie inside made Jill gasp. She had been so afraid that they were dead. Her friends and colleagues meant a great deal to her. But tempered with the pleasure of them being there alive, was the feeling of utter desolation that one of their tight-knit band could have been involved with the murder of three young kids.

As Jill, Osian and Mick stood in the doorway, they saw Eddie with a headset on and Jo with a hand on Eddie's neck.

'Oh, thank God,' Jo said. 'You've come.'

Jill could see Jo was close to complete exhaustion, both physically, mentally, and emotionally. She'd never seen Jo cry before, but silent tears were definitely wetting her cheeks. Osian quickly grabbed a chair and put it behind Jo's knees and she promptly fell into it.

'It's the game…' she said. 'It's got Eddie. He can't get the headset off until he wins the game. I can't take my hand off his neck… I'll lose my connection with him and might not get it back…'

'It's alright now, boss. We're here.' Jill looked at Osian and Mick. 'You two stay here with them, I'll go and make hot drinks.'

'Thanks, Jill, I won't leave her side,' said Mick standing behind Jo's chair with his hand on her shoulder.

'Are you alright?' Osian asked Jill. 'This is all a bit of a shock, you know.'

'Don't worry, I'm okay. Better now we've found them. You stay close to Byrd. We can't help him win the game, but we can give him support and encouragement.'

'You bet,' said Osian and moved behind Byrd and put his hand on Byrd's other shoulder.

Chapter 44

Jill burst through the door carrying a large tray which she placed on Jo's desk. On it were bottles of water, bars of chocolate and cups of sweet tea for them all. She put a hot drink into Jo's free hand so she could take a few sips.

'Nearly there now,' Jo said, whispering encouragement to Eddie. 'Nearly there my love, then we can be together.'

Jo would normally feel embarrassed about talking like that in front of Jill, Osian and her dad, but she was past caring. She just wanted Eddie out of that bloody game.

'Jo,' said Jill. 'I've got something to tell you.'
'Not now.'
'But it's important.'
'Not as important as this. Eddie must win.'
'Why?' asked Mick.
'Because if he doesn't, he'll die.'
'For real?'
'For real. Now shut up and let me concentrate.'
'You're not doing this on your own,' said Osian. 'Come on, let's form a ring, we can all fight this Penumbra thing together. That's what we've always done and we're going to do it again.'

Silently they formed a circle. With one hand on Jo's shoulder, Mick clasped Jill's hand with his other. In turn Jill held on to Osian's hand, who already had his right hand on Eddie's shoulder.

Together they forged an unbreakable bond.
Alone they were each weak and vulnerable.
Together they were a force to be reckoned with.

Chapter 45

Eddie could feel strength flowing back into his tired muscles. His fingers began to react as they had when he'd first started playing. His brain cleared of the fog of tiredness that had been filling it with cotton wool. He no longer flinched at perceived threats. He was still frightened, but now his senses were heightened. Then he felt a hand on his shoulder. Judith.

'We are all with you,' she whispered in his ear. 'You are not alone. We have forged a protective ring around you that Penumbra will find hard to break. Take whatever strength you need from us. We are here for you and will NEVER let you down. Drain us all of energy, we don't mind. We are as tall as the trees. As unyielding as stone. We are a well that you can drink from. So drink your fill. It's your destiny to be our hero.'

Eddie had never thought of himself as a hero before. He just got on and did his job. He guessed that maybe that was a bit heroic in some people's eyes. With everyone filling him with energy, it was time to turn his attention back to the game for the final push. He must get to the end. He must win.

With renewed vigour he gathered up the two boys, Masher and Prince, and in a line they turned, ready to battle Penumbra. But all was not won yet. Eddie was well aware that they had very few weapons left and that they could be easily batted away by Penumbra: the shadow who suddenly disappears, then reappears elsewhere.

'I can't do this, man,' complained Masher. 'I'm tired, thirsty and hungry. I've not got a lot left in the tank, you know?'

Eddie did know but didn't say that. Instead he said, 'Yes you can, come on, Masher, don't break now. We're so close to the end. This is the final hurdle.'

'What's so good about winning then?' asked Prince.

'Because if we don't, we die,' said Masher.

'Yeah, I get that, but why is that such a big deal?'

'Because WE really will die, not just our character,' Eddie said.

'For real?'

'For real. Now are you with me? Or do I have to do this on my own?'

Chapter 46

Eddie, Prince and Masher were tantalisingly close to the end. So much so that Eddie could almost taste victory. With Mick, Osian and Jill supporting him, Eddie could feel their energy and commitment flowing into him. In turn, the three players felt invincible, no longer afraid of their own shadows, or of any other shadow in the game.

After killing the final demon in their way, they burst into a clearing. It was then that they came face to face with Penumbra. And then that Eddie lost his nerve.

It seemed as if the game had suddenly changed from a physical game, to a mind game. Eddie started to doubt his ability. Fear took over. Would he ever get out of the game? Ever see Jo again? Ever get the damned headset off?

He looked around, helpless, but there was no support from Masher and Prince. They were still as well. Mesmerised by Penumbra.

The only movement was from their breathing. Eddie could feel their heart beats, as if they were his own and they were beating faster and faster.

Eddie was breathing in quick, shallow gasps and was in danger of hyperventilating.

And still no one moved.

Not Masher and Prince. Not Byrd.

And not Penumbra.

Chapter 47

Byrd was poised. It was now or never. Kill or be killed, their only option. He could still feel the energy of the team. He couldn't see them, but he could sense them. One by one they turned his mind around. Made him see his glass was half full and not half empty. Helped him recognised that his fear was simply mind games by Penumbra. The team's optimism was high. They had faced demons before and vanquished them.

But Byrd was well aware that Penumbra was not your usual fire and brimstone devil. This demon was much more subtle, had more finesse. Would be there one second and gone the next.

All Eddie could think to do was to fling a force-field around Penumbra, then corral him. Back him into a corner. The sort of strategy you would use to catch animals; lasso horses or put a net over dogs who were freaking out from fear. Not that Eddie thought Penumbra was frightened of them. Not at all. But he couldn't watch all three of them at the same time and as Eddie had the backing of the whole team with him, including the Church in the form of Osian, he couldn't easily be killed. Once more it was a case of good against evil. They numbered eight against one; himself, Masher, Prince, Judith, Jo, Mick, Jill and Osian.

Eddie shook himself. It was time to stop pontificating and start the last level of the game. He squared his shoulders, lifted his weapon, and said, 'Let's go boys!'

It took an agonising 15 minutes to tire out Penumbra, letting him flit here there and everywhere and then finding each player was too strong to defeat. He threw every weapon he could find at them. No one died. Every spell. No one died. He spent every gold coin he had on extra firepower. No one died. As Eddie hoped, Penumbra waned, his energy spent, his weapons empty, until he lay on the floor, on his back, within their unbreakable circle. Eddie lifted his sword high. Then plunged it into Penumbra's heart. It was over. They had triumphed. They had lived. Lived to play again another day.

Eddie thanked the two players, Prince and Masher, and grinned as they whooped in triumph. He was about to rip the headset off, when a gif appeared, a silhouette of a man, all in black, clad in a cloak, clapping them. Penumbra acknowledging their win. Byrd smiled. But then frowned. Something about it was familiar. There was something about the features. Then he realised who it was. Who was really behind this game and the deaths.

Chapter 48

At long last the game was over and Jo could relax. Maybe not so much relax, as collapse. Taking her hand off Eddie's neck, she slumped in her chair. Then Jill pressed another mug of hot sweet tea in her hand.

'Come on, boss,' Jill said. 'You must drink this.'

Jo nodded mutely and she watched Eddie rip the headset off as he blinked and looked around at their little group.

'I did it?' he asked.

'Yes, you did,' replied Jo. Tears threatened and as she lost control of her emotions, they ran unchecked down her cheeks. The relief was overwhelming.

Then Eddie said, 'I know who it is.'

'Who who is?' sniffed Jo. 'What the hell are you talking about? Please don't speak in riddles, my poor brain can't handle it.'

'Penumbra.'

'So do I,' said Jill.

Jo was confused still. 'What? What the hell is going on, you two. Come on, let's have it, who is Penumbra then?'

As one, Eddie and Jill said, 'Sasha.'

'What? You must be mad, both of you,' said Jo, not understanding at all. 'How can it be Sasha? I know she's a computer geek, and socially inept, but really, writing a computer game that kills people? Surely not.'

With every mouthful of the hot drink, Jo was feeling better. And now she had something else to concentrate on, instead of her fear of Eddie dying, which was good. But still, Sasha?

'Right, Jill, let's start with you. Back up your theory of it being Sasha.'

'Well, Osian came round last night for supper,' Jill blushed and glanced at her fiancé, making Jo smile.

'And?' she prompted.

'Oh, sorry, and he saw the Penumbra logo in my papers. I'd been re-reading my file in case something jogged my memory. You know, helped in any way. So, anyway, Osian saw it and said he'd seen that somewhere before. This morning he rang as he'd remembered where. It was on one of Sasha's notebooks. She saw him looking at it and quickly covered it up.'

'She looked really guilty,' Osian piped up. 'It was all very odd.'

Jo nodded. 'And Eddie?'

'At the end of the game, the silhouette turns to face the player who has beaten him. But it's not a man.'

'It looks like Sasha?'

'Yes. The ultimate ego trip, I guess, putting your own features on your character.'

'Evil character,' interjected Jill.

'Evil character,' Eddie conceded. 'So what do you think?' he asked Jo.

'I think we better find her. Come on,' and Jo began to get up.

'Woah, no you don't,' said Mick. 'Look at you two, you're dead on your feet. The only place you're going is out for breakfast with me.'

'But we have to find her,' protested Jo, even though she knew her father was probably right.

'Jill and Osian can go after Sasha,' he said. 'Jo, I'm not asking, I'm telling.'

'Oh my God,' laughed Jo, 'you're pulling rank on me!'

'Damn right I am,' he grinned. 'Well, what are you waiting for?' he barked to Jill and Osian.

'Oh, right, sorry, come on, Osian.'

Chapter 49

'Where do we start?' Osian asked Jill.

'Let's try her phones first.'

Jill took her mobile and Osian her home phone. There was no reply from either.

'Come on then, let's go to her flat.'

But Jill didn't go to the car park, she left by the front entrance to the police station and started walking. Osian asked where they were going.

'Roman quarter.'

'Ooh, nice,' said Osian. 'Very swish as well, just by the ancient city walls and only a few minutes walk to the town centre. I've always admired those apartments. Don't they have a concierge service as well?'

'Some of them,' said Jill. 'But I don't think Sasha's had.'

They were soon in the Roman quarter and Jill checked the address she'd stored in her phone. 'Come on, it's this one,' she said to Osian and once inside the complex they took the lift to the 2nd floor.

They stepped into a corridor that was straight out of a hotel. Thick carpets lined the hallway and the front doors looked sturdy and modern. Jill stopped outside apartment 2C. As she rapped on the door it swung open.

'That's strange,' she said. 'It's not locked.'

'It's not even closed,' said Osian as he watched

the door open to reveal the inside of the apartment.

'Sasha?' called Jill. 'Are you in?'

When there was no response, Osian and Jill ventured inside. To find – nothing.

'There's nothing here,' breathed Osian.

'It doesn't make sense,' said Jill as they walked around. 'There nothing much in here. Bare walls. Bare rooms. All of them empty.'

'Did she really live here do you think?' asked Osian.

'Let's ask the neighbours.'

There was no reply to their knock at 2A, but a disgruntled, heavily made-up woman answered the door at 2B.

'Oh, her,' she said, to Jill's enquiry about her neighbour. 'Comes and goes at all hours of the day and night. Bloody nuisance really. She wakes the dog, who barks and wakes me,' she indicated her yappy miniature Yorkshire terrier at her heels. 'And she wasn't chatty. Never said much, in fact never said anything at all come to think of it.'

'But she definitely lived here?'

'Oh, yes.'

'Her hours were probably erratic as she worked for the police,' said Jill.

'Oh, was that what it was? I thought she was into computers.'

'Well she is. Why?'

'The flat was full of equipment.'

'Really?'

'Yes, I called round once to complain.'

'And?'

'And the door was open so I walked in, trying to find her. I saw inside the front room. All sorts of stuff in there, computers, oh and those funny headset things, like something out of Star Trek. Gave me the creeps I can tell you.'

'When did you last hear her?' asked Osian.

'Yesterday afternoon. A van pulled up late afternoon and she started loading all her stuff into it. Hopefully, she's gone for good and I can get some peace.'

'Were there any markings on the van?'

'No, just a white van.'

'No hire company? Removal company?'

'No, sorry.'

'Was anyone helping her?' asked Osian.

'No, it was just her and good riddance I can tell you. I've had quite enough,' and she slammed the door in their faces.

Chapter 50

Jo had just chosen what she wanted to eat from the café's menu, when Osian and Jill turned up to report their findings, or rather lack of them.

'She's gone,' said a dejected Osian. 'The flat was empty. A neighbour saw her moving out last night.'

'Shit,' said Jo.

'Do you think you'll find her?' asked Mick.

'No,' Jo shook her head. 'She's too good. She'll have covered her tracks well.'

'She's probably got another identity all set up ready to go. She knows how to play the game, what with her insider knowledge,' said Eddie.

Jo nodded. 'She's a ghost. A shadow. A Penumbra.'

'What if she does it again?' asked Jill.

'She won't risk it, she knows we'll set up alerts.'

'Do you think she meant to kill people?' asked Mick. 'I never met her, so I don't have an opinion.'

'I don't know. I hope not.'

That would make Jo feel doubly betrayed. It was bad enough that someone she'd really tried to help had turned out to be rotten to the core.

Jo remembered how she'd rescued Sasha from the bullying and name-calling of her male colleagues. She'd given Sasha a chance, welcomed her into the team after Judith died. And for what? To be stabbed in the back. Sasha nearly killed Eddie for God's sake. Jo didn't think she'd ever forgive Sasha's treachery.

'More likely that she wanted to make her fortune,' said Byrd. 'Isn't that what all gamers want? To come up with the ultimate game?'

'Well, I'm not leaving it, boss,' said Jill and began to gather her stuff.

'Where are you off to?' asked Osian.

'To check CCTV. Maybe I can find the white van.'

'To see if WE can find it, you mean.'

'Don't you have work to do at the Cathedral?' asked Jill.

'Oh no, I'm having far too much fun here,' and he grinned round at everyone.

Jill looked at Jo, who nodded her permission. 'Welcome to the team,' she said to Osian. 'You are now officially a police consultant.'

'A temporary police consultant,' said Jill.

'Oh, don't be so picky,' said Osian. 'Come on then, what are we waiting for?'

As Jill and Osian walked away, Jo heard Jill warn him, 'It's pretty boring you know, going through CCTV footage.'

'Yes, but think how exciting it will be when we find her!'

Osian was clearly unbowed by the thought of going through hours of CCTV and Jo smiled at the pair's happiness at the opportunity to work together once more.

'I think we need to grab a few hours' sleep after

this food,' said Byrd as the waitress approached with their meals. 'I don't know about you, but I've just about had it.'

'Alright,' said Jo. 'Here,' and she handed him the car keys. 'You can drive.'

Chapter 51

As Jill opened the door to the CCTV suite of offices, Osian stopped and looked around in wonder. In a large open-plan office there were officers and technicians working away watching archive CCTV footage on large monitors. But it was the sight at the end of the room that had caught his attention. That was where officers watched the CCTV images in real time. In the control room was a wall of 50 or so monitors capturing images from streets and parks across Chichester and the wider area.

'Wow,' he said. 'I've never seen anything like it. Talk about Big Brother is watching.'

'I know, it's a shock when you first see it, isn't it? The cameras are monitored 24 hours a day, with officers looking for suspicious and criminal activity. They retain all footage for 31 days.'

'What are they looking for?'

'Detection and prevention of crime, ultimately. And it's also for the reassurance of the general public.'

'I never realised there were so many cameras,' Osian said. 'You walk around and never notice them. Are there any around the Cathedral?'

'Yes, loads, we need to keep all our lovely tourists safe, and those in the congregation and the clergy, of course.'

'Me? You mean they'll have cameras on me?'

'Well, not you specifically, but yes, I guess

you'd feature quite often.'

'I'm not sure I like the thought of that,' said Osian with a shudder.

'Look at it another way,' said Jill. 'If the operators notice criminal activity on camera in or around the Cathedral, they direct police response to the incident. So it's' a prevention and detection system that works really well. Imagine there was a knife carrying youth stalking you. It would be noticed by the control room staff and police sent to arrest the youth and keep you safe.'

Osian rubbed his chin. 'Well, I suppose, when you put it like that...'

'They do their utmost to safeguard our most vulnerable citizens as well, whether they are young people or old people. They could see someone who's ill and call for assistance. Someone who's sleeping rough and having their belongings taken and call for assistance. It's not just about catching criminals all the time.'

'I guess not,' he said. 'So what happens now?'

'Now we go to the Control Room Supervisor and get access to the CCTV system covering Sasha's last known whereabouts.'

'Her flat in the Roman Quarter.'

'Yes, come on, let's do it. Jo and Eddie are trusting us to find Sasha and we can't let them down.'

'Absolutely not,' said Osian with renewed vigour. 'Lead the way.'

Slowly the minutes turned into hours and the

hours ticked away towards the end of the day before Jill was satisfied that they'd done everything they could to find Sasha. Finally they walked away from the monitors. Their eyes felt like they were out on stalks, Jill had a headache coming and Osian had lost his fascination with the CCTV suite hours before. They returned to the police station, with welcome take-away coffees for everyone.

'Feeling better?' Jill asked Jo and Eddie as they handed the coffees around.

'Loads, thanks.'

Jill wished she did. By now she was pretty dead on her feet. But she had the feeling that her day wasn't going to end any time soon, not with the news they had for Jo and Eddie.

'So, what have you got for us?'

Jill loaded the appropriate CCTV images into her computer and then displayed them on their large monitor.

'Right, here's the van turning into Sasha's building and leaving again what three hours later? So we can surmise she packed her belongings in that van.'

'We followed her from the Roman Quarter to the ring road,' said Osian proudly. 'I found her there,' he said allowing himself a moment of pride.

Eddie grinned, 'Well done you!'

Osian acknowledged the praise.

'This is where she turned off the A27,' Jill said, indicating the road to Boxgrove. Then she joins the A285 and that's the last sighting at the junction in Halnaker. I'm afraid there's no CCTV from there.'

'What time was that?'

'About 11pm last night.'

Jo looked at her watch. 'It's getting dark now, so let's get the helicopter up over there with a thermal imaging camera on it. Tonight. As soon as they can. Meanwhile, Eddie, get a team together. I want us all ready to go in an hour.'

'Yes, boss,' Eddie said and picked up his mobile. 'Armed?'

'Yes, better to be safe than sorry, don't you think? After all, in my book, Sasha is a murderer.'

Chapter 52

Jo, Byrd, Jill and Osian had followed the trail up to Halnaker. The question was, where had she gone from there. She hadn't continued up the A285 because they didn't pick her up on the cameras there, so she must have turned off at Halnaker towards Goodwood. They met the armed response team close to a property out in the countryside near Goodwood racecourse. They were parked in a small layby about 100 yards from the building, under the lea of a large hedgerow, which hid them from the house. There was only one dim light that they could see on in the property, which they thought was in the kitchen. All the other windows appeared to be covered over by tightly closed curtains. They were unsure as to whether Sasha was alone in the cottage, or there with co-conspirators.

'Don't forget that she could be armed and dangerous,' cautioned Jo.

'Really?' said Jill. 'I'm sorry but I can't see Sasha being a killer.'

'I think it's because we don't want to,' said Byrd. 'Don't forget what happened to the boys from Dynamic Developments. They were badly mutilated. If they hadn't been found quickly, they would have died. It's likely that was either Sasha or an accomplice.'

'Do you think it could have been done accidentally?'

'No. You'll have to trust me on that one, Osian,' said Byrd. 'You didn't see them.'

'Why? What happened to them?'

Jo kicked Byrd's ankle as a warning to be careful what he said.

'Let's just say they won't be helping us with our enquiries anytime soon.'

Jill saw Osian's brow furrow in confusion and so she quickly changed the subject before he started asking more awkward questions. 'What's with the house, boss?' asked Jill. 'Why have you chosen this one and why is it empty?'

'Someone murdered their whole family in it,' Jo explained. 'Shot his mother, father and sister with a sawn-off shotgun, would you believe. Then he just sat there in a rocking chair in the kitchen surrounded by their bodies, until the police came and arrested him.'

'Surely you have to be mentally ill to do something like that,' said Osian.

'I'd call it deranged,' said Eddie.

'Where is he now?'

'Broadmoor secure mental hospital.'

'And we think that farm is where Sasha is holed up?'

'Yes, it's as good a guess as any. As I said we know the building is abandoned. It stands alone, surrounded by countryside the nearest neighbour probably half a mile away. No one wants to buy it, or live in it, due to its history. The thermal camera shows there is someone in it now, though. There are lots more indicators that there is something in a barn next to the house. It could be her equipment, as that heat source is stationary, whereas the thermal trace in the house keeps moving around.'

Jo went over to the armed response team commander. 'Ready?'

He nodded. 'Whenever you are.'

'Okay, let's move out.'

They collected by the five-bar wooden gate at the entrance to the farm. A police officer opened the gate, his feet crunching on the gravel underfoot, and held it until they had all passed through. Jo was worried about the amount of noise they were making. If Sasha, or someone else, were keeping a look out, they would already have heard the encroaching police officers.

The whole team fanned out on the grass and gingerly walked towards the house. They displayed no lights and for the moment their radios were on 'silent'. Once at the building they all lined up against the wall of the cottage, taking care not to pass any windows. The team commander raised his arm and they held their collected breaths. As he pulled it down, the signal to go in, an officer who was stood by the door, responded by breaking it down with a battering ram. The armed response team streamed into the house shouting, 'Armed police. Armed police. On the floor. NOW!'

Jo walked in behind them, to find Sasha splayed

out on the quarry tiles laid on the floor of the kitchen, her hands on her head. Jo nodded to Eddie who walked over and put the handcuffs on her and read Sasha her rights. He pulled her up, so she was standing in front of Jo, her head bowed, hiding behind her hair.

Jo looked at the woman she had befriended and said, 'How could you?'

When Jo didn't receive a reply, she turned on her heel and walked away.

Chapter 53

Osian and Jill had gone home for a well-deserved rest. Interviewing Sasha would be down to Jo and Byrd. Not that Jo was looking forward to it. She still felt betrayed by Sasha. To Jo it was unforgivable what Sasha had done. Putting people at risk like that. What sort of monster would you have to be to devise a game where if your character died, you did too? It was beyond her understanding. It made Sasha no better than any of the supernatural beings Jo and Byrd fought. Jo and Byrd stood for good. Sasha and her ilk stood for evil. In Jo's book it was that simple.

Jo looked through the two-way mirror. Sasha was sat at a metal table, which was bolted to the floor. Her hands lay on top of it. Her head was bowed and her hair hung down like curtains and covered her face. She'd barely moved in the past hour.

'Ready?' she asked the police officer who was in charge of the recording equipment. There was audio and video set up which would be monitored whilst the interview took place.

At his nod she said, 'Come on then,' to Byrd. 'Let's do this.'

With a heart as heavy as the boots on her feet, Jo entered the small interview room and excused the officer waiting by the door. Jo and Byrd sat opposite Sasha, who still hadn't lifted her head. Byrd began the interview by noting the time, and the participants and confirmed that Sasha had waived her right to legal representation.

'Sasha,' Jo began. 'I've only got one question. Why? Why did you make such an appalling game?'

'I didn't mean for anyone to die,' said Sasha. 'I didn't know that was going to happen.'

'Sasha,' Jo said moderating her voice, trying hard for calm and reasonable. 'Look at me, Sasha.'

As Sasha lifted her head, she looked at Jo with sorrow in her red-rimmed, swollen eyes. It was all very well crying, Jo thought. But it was rather too little too late. 'Will you explain what happened?'

'It wasn't me. I didn't make people die. You have to believe me.'

Jo had to admit that Sasha struck a pitiful sight. In police custody, destined to spend the rest of her life behind bars and never being given access to a computer again, was the future that stretched out before her.

'If it wasn't you, who was it? Help me understand what went wrong. Who else is behind this?'

Haltingly Sasha spoke. 'It was Penumbra himself. At least that's what he's always called himself. We met at university and a couple of years ago he persuaded me to help him with coding a new game. He said we would make our fortune. I don't make much money working for the police you know. A lot of work for not a lot of money got to me in the end and I agreed to do it. I never should have listened to her. I never should have trusted her.'

Tears welled in Sasha's eyes, but Jo didn't have much sympathy for the girl. As far as she was concerned you joined the police to prevent evil, not actively assist it. You couldn't just turn away from your responsibility to uphold the law. You didn't get to pick and choose. It was all or nothing. Black or white. No grey. She said as much to Sasha.

'I know, that's why she had to do it and not me.'

'Sasha, you're not making any sense.'

'Who are you talking about?' asked Byrd.

'Her. Strike.'

'Strike?'

'Yes, I didn't want to do it, so Strike did it. She told me what a bloody sissy I was. A frightened freak, she called me.'

'Sasha, who the hell is Strike?'

But Sasha just shook her head.

'Where can we find her? What does she look like?'

Sasha put her arms around herself, began crying again and rocking.

'For God's sake,' said Byrd. 'This is ridiculous. We're getting nowhere,' and he went to leave the room in disgust. 'Are you coming, Jo?'

She was just about to follow Byrd, when someone said, 'Oooh, get you, Mr Policeman.'

Jo and Byrd whirled round, both clearly confused as to who had spoken. The voice sounded like Sasha, but was deeper and with attitude. As Jo watched, Sasha sat up and scraped her hair off her face, tying it in some sort of knot.

Head held high she said, 'You two really do think you're the dog's bollocks, don't you?'

'Sasha?' said Jo.

'What the hell?' asked Byrd.

'Strike, actually. Don't take any notice of stupid Sasha, retard that she is. All quiet and shy like a little mouse. You don't really think she could do anything like that, do you? I'm the one prepared to take risks, live a little, you know? So I wrote the game, not her,' she sneered. 'And Penumbra did the headsets, not that moron Fielding. He was just a gopher really. He's not worth the time of day.'

'Fielding?' Jo wondered who was going mad. Her or Sasha, or all of them. She felt like she'd dropped into the set of One Flew Over the Cuckoo's Nest.

'Sasha,' Byrd said, ignoring Strike and her attitude, trying to get back the girl he knew. 'Did you mutilate the boys from Dynamic Developments? Pluck out their eyes so they couldn't see you. Cut out their tongues so they couldn't tell the police about you? Or was that Strike as well?'

Byrd was clearly going for shock tactics. Jo couldn't blame him. They were both still reeling from the revelations in this case, and they badly needed answers, quickly.

'Me? Of course not!' Sasha's head jerked up. She was back. 'How could you think that?'

'Sasha, to be honest I don't know what to think anymore. You're not the person I thought you were,' said Byrd.

Or was it people, Jo wondered? In the plural.

'What's Penumbra's name?' Jo gently asked.

'Michael Fielding.'

'And where does he live?'

Sasha gave them an address in Littlehampton. 'But I've not been able to raise him,' said Sasha. 'I don't know what's happened to him. If he's still there, even.'

'Alright. That'll do for now,' said Jo, standing up. 'I'll get someone to escort you back to the cells, but we'll want to speak to you again.'

Chapter 54

Jo and Byrd tumbled out of the interview room door and leaned against the wall in the corridor.

'Strike?' said Byrd. 'What the hell?'

'I think she's an alter,' said Jo shaking her head. 'Poor Sasha.'

'Poor Sasha! Are you serious?'

'I think Sasha is ill. She could have a condition where she has multiple personalities, DID they call it now, I believe. Dissociative identity disorder. Strike must be an alter, or alternative personality.'

'Really?'

'Really. So I'm afraid we can't interview her any further. It's necessary to get her seen by a doctor at the very least, but preferably a psychiatrist. I believe the out of character behaviour we've just witnessed is the result of an alternate identity being in control. Let's get one of the staff to get her a doctor and then we need to go after this Michael Fielding.'

Jo once more assembled the team of armed response officers.

'This time,' she informed the team leader, 'we're going after a second individual involved in this case. By all accounts Sasha and this Michael Fielding worked together on the development and coding of the game.'

'Do we know if he'll be alone?'

'No. I'm sorry I don't have more information and appreciate we're going in blind. Which is why I want you on hand.'

He nodded his agreement.

'Thanks. We'll be ready to go in ten minutes.'

Jo looked at Eddie who seemed close to dropping. 'Why don't you go home,' she said. 'You look dead on your feet.'

But Eddie refused. 'I'm the one who beat him in the game, remember. Maybe I have to be the one to beat him in the flesh as well.'

Jo couldn't fault that logic, so off they went.

Chapter 55

As they drove to Littlehampton, Eddie filled Jo in on the property they were going to. 'It looks like Michael Fielding lives above a computer shop. Probably his. It doesn't have many good reviews, mind,' he said. 'It seems customer service and reasonable prices aren't his forte.'

'It's probably a front,' said Jo and Byrd nodded his agreement.

Jo, Eddie, and the armed response officers congregated in a small carpark. The computer shop was located at the beginning of the pedestrian-only shopping area. Normally, especially on market day, this collection of shops would be very busy with shoppers out looking for bargains. On sunny days, the terraces of the independent coffee houses would be rammed with tourists and locals alike. But now, in the middle of the night, all the shops were securely locked tight and no one roamed the deserted streets. Even the homeless were more than likely fast asleep in the doorways.

As they walked around the corner into the pedestrianised street, Jo spotted the shop opposite them. In the sodium light it looked in a sorry state. The wooden window frames were rotting away in places, old, sun-bleached posters filled the windows. They were all protected by a chain-link security grill pulled down and secured by a padlock. Next to the door to the shop, was another door, clearly leading upstairs to the flat above.

The team leader looked at Jo and she nodded to him. It was the signal to get on with it. With an ear-splitting crash the battering ram demolished the rotting door, revealing stairs leading upward to the flat. Once more the officers burst into a property shouting, 'Armed police, armed police, get down on the floor NOW!'

When Jo and Eddie walked into what she supposed could be loosely called a living room, they found a man of around 30 slumped in a chair.

'He won't get on the ground, ma'am,' the team leader said. 'Shall we make him?'

Jo looked at the floor. A black carpet was swirled through with an old-fashioned pattern. As she walked, it felt sticky underfoot. She wasn't sure that anyone had ever cleaned it. Over by the window was a strip that was vivid red and black. Something had recently stood there and kept the carpet clean underneath it. A testament to how dirty the carpet was now. Jo shrugged, 'I wouldn't want to get down on that, either.'

As Eddie followed Jo into the room, Fielding pointed and said, 'You! You and your loser pals have ruined everything. Why couldn't you just die like everyone else?'

'That was your objective then? For people to really die?' asked Eddie.

'Of course, you moron. Why else?' Fielding's voice was changing. Becoming louder and deeper, with an echoing quality to it. The kind of voice that filled

nightmares and Jo shivered as the air in the flat, not warm to begin with, began to plunge in temperature.

Without warning, Fielding sprang from the chair and appeared to morph into someone or something else.

Jo had the impression of a very tall figure. Shadowy. As black as the night. As cold as ice.

As he loomed over them, Jo could just make out the silhouette of a man with a cloak on.

'Who are you?' Jo screwed up all her courage so as to not sound frightened, or hesitant, or weak. Especially weak. Demons liked weakness. They prised open cracks in your psyche, slithering down them, deep into your soul. So she stood tall and resolute.

'I'm your worst nightmare. The shadow you can't see coming. The evil in the cellar. The beast behind the locked door.'

With each sentence the being became larger, denser. He seemed to draw strength from their presence and Jo began to feel lightheaded and somewhat confused. She frowned, as the beginning of a headache threatened behind her eyes.

The room was becoming ever darker, shadows from the corners lengthening and creeping towards them. Penumbra spun his cloak around in the air, covering Jo and Eddie. A muffling blanket seemed to envelop them. Jo's hearing became muffled and she sought out Byrd who was looking confused and disoriented, shaking his head as if to clear it, to no avail. She couldn't make eye contact with him and cried out as she watched him crumble to the floor.

As Penumbra took a menacing step towards Jo, she could only watch in horror as his cloak of black draped itself over her and Byrd.

An officer behind her cried out in fear. The crack of a shot caused Jo to scream and Fielding fell to the floor. Jo watched as the black demon turned into whisps of black smoke and then dispersed, streaming out through the cracks in the old wooden window frame. As the air cleared and lightened, Jo looked around her, trying to find a glimpse of the demon. But only a few shadows remained in the flat in the corners of the room and outside the window was the still, black night. The demon was gone. Who knew where?

When she turned back to the room, Eddie was kneeling on the floor next to Fielding. 'It looks like he's been shot in the head,' he said, putting two fingers to Fielding's neck. 'But he's still alive!'

As Jo looked up, the team leader nodded and pressed a button on the side of his radio. He summoned the ambulance from where it had been waiting in the car park. His eyes were full of questions, but as Jo shook her head he turned on his heel and ushered his men from the building.

Chapter 56

Jo and Eddie followed the ambulance to the hospital. Jo had asked that the patient be taken to Chichester, rather than Worthing, as it was closer for the police to be able to keep an eye on their suspect. And anyway, Jo didn't want any other force knowing of the existence of her unit.

The paramedics determined that there was no immediate threat to Fielding's life. The bleed from his head had been staunched and from what they could tell he was in a coma. For the sake of an extra few miles, they complied. After all, Chichester was a larger hospital with more facilities for looking after patients with head wounds, which was what ultimately swayed their decision.

Once at Chichester hospital, Jo and Byrd took the time to get a coffee and a something to eat while Fielding was being examined and admitted.

'So what happened there?' asked Eddie as they collected their drinks and sat down in the hospital café.

'I think we can agree that Fielding was possessed by an entity, Penumbra. And that is what we saw flee Fielding's body when he was shot.'

'Agreed,' said Byrd. 'So what's next?'

'Sorry?'

'What's next as far as this entity, Penumbra is concerned?'

'Ah.'

'Ah? That's not very helpful.'

'It's all I've got. It may find someone else to possess. It could have cut and run back to wherever it came from. I really don't know, Byrd. All we can say for sure is that we saw it leave Fielding's body when he was shot.'

'This whole fighting demons thing isn't as straightforward as you'd think, is it?'

'No, it's not,' agreed Jo.

'Ever had the feeling we're making it up as we go along?'

Jo grinned. 'Most definitely. All I can say for now is that Penumbra is out of Fielding and hopefully out of the game.'

'Not that anyone else will be playing it. I take it we'll now issue a warning through the press and social media, recalling the game and the headsets?'

'Exactly. So let's be thankful for small mercies, eh?'

As soon as they were full of reviving caffeine and sugar, they went up to the Intensive Care Unit, where they met the duty Consultant, who had been examining Fielding in a private room.

'How is he, doctor?' asked Jo.

'As well as can be expected. Nothing can be done for him at the moment. A scan has revealed that the bullet is lodged in his brain, and there is slight swelling in the area due to the trauma. I want him monitored over the next few hours. If the brain continues to swell, we may need to perform an operation to take the pressure off. But as I said, the best course of action is to leave things alone for now and monitor him closely. The neurosurgeon is saying that as the bullet velocity was high and there was no side to side movement of the head and it passed through non-critical parts of the patient's brain, then survival is possible.'

'Will he regain consciousness?'

'I don't know. He's in a coma. Who knows what the outcome will be? I'm afraid these things take time. He may recover. He may not. That's the best I can give you for now.'

Jo took a moment, looking down on Fielding handcuffed to the bed. Wondering what was going on in the man's mind. She'd shuddered when she had first seen him lying in the ambulance, in a coma. Jo knew all about comas. How the mind and body shut down to protect itself. Tried to heal itself from the inside out. Fielding could well recover. She did. Mind you, she hadn't had a bullet in her brain. A horse's hoof marked the spot of her own injury and she subconsciously rubbed at the scar on her temple.

Byrd must have seen her, as he said, 'Come on, Jo,' and he put his arm around her shoulder. 'Let's get out of here.'

She nodded and encased in his arm, allowed him to lead her out of the room. As they left, a policeman took their place and sat by the side of Fielding's bed.

The officer pulled a small paperback book out of his pocket and started to read. He was a few pages in and engrossed in the story when, unnoticed, the shadows started to collect in the corners of the room, gaining strength, filling the room with whisps of darkness. The officer's mobile was in his pocket, the ringer turned off. As he continued to read his novel, the light turned on on the phone. Then, with slow deliberation a number was keyed in. There was a pause, then the mobile connected with the number dialled.

Chapter 57

Jo sent Byrd home and went to see Sasha in her police cell. The duty doctor had been to see her and she was awaiting transport to a secure mental unit in a nearby hospital where she would undergo tests to see if she was a danger to herself and if she was mentally competent enough to stand trial. Jo asked for Sasha's cell door to be opened.

'Ma'am?' frowned the Sergeant in charge.

'Just a conversation,' said Jo. 'You can stay if you want.'

After a pause, he nodded and unlocked the door.

Jo leaned against the open door and said, 'Sasha, when did you realise what was going on with the game? That something was truly wrong?'

Sasha looked up at Jo, through the curtain of her hair. 'When we got the case that young Callum was dead. And then when Jill found more cases, I couldn't ignore it any longer. I went to see Fielding.'

'And?'

'It wasn't him.'

'What do you mean?'

'Whoever it was that I talked to, wasn't Fielding. It was as if he'd been taken over by someone else.'

'Or something else?' said Jo.

'Exactly. Oh I'm so glad you understand. I

didn't know what to do. I was told to go away and not tell anyone what I'd seen or heard.'

'And what had you seen.'

'Fielding change somehow. He became taller, blacker, like a shadow. Like the shadow Penumbra in the game. He paced around speaking to me. His words were chilling. He said I would suffer a fate worse than death if I didn't keep what I knew about him and the game, to myself. And then Fielding was back, but he refused to speak to me. Turned his chair around so he had his back to me. After pleading with him to tell me how this had happened and how we could get out of it, I still didn't get any response. So I had no choice but to leave.'

'Sasha,' Jo moved to sit on the small bed, next to Sasha. 'Can you tell me what it feels like to be you?' Jo asked. 'I want to understand. Please.'

'Having a dissociative disorder means that I haven't been myself for a long time,' Sasha said. 'I feel like a mimic of myself. I'm a person trying my best to play 'me', when I haven't been properly briefed on who it is I'm meant to be playing. It's confusing to say the least. That's the best way to describe it I think.'

'And what happens?'

'How do you mean?'

'When another you is in charge. How does that feel?'

'Sometimes my head gets full of cotton wool that clogs it up. I can feel disconnected from my surroundings, as if I am seeing the world in a dreamlike state. The biggest problem I've found in everyday life with dissociative disorder is social interaction. I find speaking to others and holding a conversation very stressful. But that's when I'm me.'

Jo nodded. She had seen that, as had many others in the police station. Jo had always thought that Sasha had some sort of autism. But maybe not.

'When Strike's in charge, then I'm completely different. She's completely different. Let's face it, she was the one who was on show for most of my time at university. I had disassociated. Disappeared under the force of Strike's personality. She's the complete opposite of me.'

'I can see that from the short discussion I've had with her.'

'She's never appeared in the police station before. I think that must give you an idea of how frightened I am. Strike is the more forceful character. She likes to take charge and get things done. I don't mean to come across stand-offish, but because of my symptoms, I often do. I can't help it. I have tried explaining to others why I act a bit odd sometimes, but the subject makes them uncomfortable. It can be very isolating.'

'What should we do?' asked Jo, genuinely interested.

'The best thing to do, if someone is acting stand-offish or in a way you consider to be strange, is to be kind to them by treating them normally. Don't take the way they are acting personally. I often find that when I am at my worst, is when I get a bad reaction from others, which is the opposite of what I need. Being treated like there is something wrong with you only makes it more isolating and distressing. You're the only one who has ever cared enough to do that for me. Treat me like I was normal, I mean.'

'And the boys from DD? Was that their warning?'

'Oh, God,' Sasha covered her face with her hands. 'I think that was a warning to me, either from Fielding or Penumbra. To show me what would happen if I spoke up.'

'It was a very graphic warning.'

Sasha nodded. 'I was truly terrified. All I could think about was getting away.'

'So you did a moonlight flit, as my grandmother would say.'

Sasha looked confused.

'Left without telling anyone,' Jo clarified.

'Yes, but it didn't work, did it? I should have known you lot would find me. What happens now?'

'That depends on the doctors. You're being taken to a secure mental unit for evaluation. You won't get bail, you know.'

Sasha nodded. 'Because I ran.'

'Because you ran. And because of the severity of your crimes, of course.'

Suddenly Jo couldn't wait to get out of the claustrophobic space and she stood, turned on her heel and strode out of the cell without another word. Taking deep breaths of air, she left the police station. It was time for her to go home to Byrd.

Chapter 58

Masher collapsed on the bed. He was mentally and emotionally drained. No one must know how close he'd come to dying. His mum would have a fit and his dad would throw away all his equipment, especially that awesome headset. No, it must be protected at all costs. For despite the tiredness there was exaltation. They had won. They'd beaten Penumbra. How cool was that?

He wondered what had happened to Penumbra? He'd seemed so real, tantalisingly real and it took three of them to kill him. Or at least he thought they'd killed him. They must have, they'd finished the game and taken their headsets off. Or he could have just let them win so he could get away to come back another day. Either way, it wasn't really his problem. What he needed now was rest. He lay down and closed his eyes, but it didn't work. He was still wide awake. His head a jumble of thoughts, scenes from the game, the feeling of being stalked re-lived. Everything was bouncing through his mind.

Then his phone buzzed, zooming across the bedside table.

He picked it up and answered it.

'Want to play?' a disembodied voice whispered.

Masher grinned in the dark.

Then left the bed, turned on his lamp and his

laptop.

And slipped the headset on.

THE END

From the author

I do hope you've enjoyed following DI Jo Wolfe and her team on their supernatural adventures. They'll be back with more cases in 2021.

While you're waiting, why not try a book from one of my other series, starting with the Sgt Major Crane crime thriller, Steps to Heaven? Click on the covers to go to your local Amazon store.

Rebus meets Reacher in Sgt Major Crane...
A soldier and his family lie dead in their own home. Why? No one knows. But to Crane, it's looking more like murder every day.
Then it happens to another family. Same circumstances. Different location.
When the Garrison Padre is kidnapped, Crane and DI Anderson of the Aldershot Police unearth a sinister figure hiding in the shadows, reshaping everything Crane thought he knew about soldier's minds - and his own.
When at last the shocking truth becomes clear... is Crane too late to save his soldiers and their children?

If you've read those books, there's always the Crane and Anderson series, beginning with Death Rites. Click on the covers to go to your local Amazon store.

The disappearance of young girls. An investigation hindered by a new member of the team. Can Crane survive the case with his body and mind intact?
With Aldershot gripped by the case of missing young girls, the relentless detectives DI Anderson and Sgt Major Crane uncover a coven of evil worshipers. And so the two men embark on a perilous journey to catch an evil serial killer in their midst. But when all seems lost, Crane refuses to give in. Even as he finds that you don't have to die... to go to hell.

There will also be a series of cosy mystery short reads coming in 2021. It's going to be a busy year!

Until next time,
Happy Reading!